WHAT'S THE COST OF FAME?

I hear the engines turn off, and the silence is like a sacred hush after all the noise of the day. I barely wake for it, just notice it in passing, like I notice Joshua's quiet weight and heat beside me.

The waves rock me right back to sleep.

In my dream, I hover above the night-dark ocean. I'm flying, spinning through the air like Lillian Leitzel. I sense Joshua with me, moving in the air somewhere, but I can't see him. So I spin and flutter, weightless.

Then something unseen snaps. A sudden break like a gunshot, jarring my arm, and suddenly the air can't hold me anymore.

I plummet, the wind snatching the screams from my mouth. I flail into empty air, reaching for something, for hands, for a harness, for a net.

Nothing will save me.

As I hit the water, I jerk awake, heart drumming with a jolt of inhalation. I feel cold and sweaty at the same time.

I reach out for Joshua, for the feel of something solid, real.

The air around me is empty. The mattress beside me is cool to the touch.

Joshua is gone.

ALSO BY ASH PARSONS

Still Waters

Girls Save the World in This One

OTHER BOOKS YOU MAY ENJOY

Things I'm Seeing Without You	Peter Bognanni
Lies You Never Told Me	Jennifer Donaldson
The First Time She Drowned	Kerry Kletter
We Are Okay	Nina LaCour

Holding on to You

ASH PARSONS

PENGUIN BOOKS

FOR ALL WHO STRUGGLE.

YOU'RE NOT ALONE.

PENGUIN BOOKS
An imprint of Penguin Random House LLC, New York

First published in the United States of America as *The Falling Between Us*
by Philomel Books, an imprint of Penguin Random House LLC, 2018
Published by Penguin Books, an imprint of Penguin Random House LLC, 2020.

Visit us online at penguinrandomhouse.com

Philomel Books is a registered trademark of Penguin Random House LLC.

LIBRARY OF CONGRESS CATALOGING-IN-PUBLICATION DATA IS AVAILABLE.

Penguin Books ISBN 9780147512123

Printed in the United States of America.

10 9 8 7 6 5 4 3 2 1

Edited by Michael Green.
Design by Ellice Lee.
Text set in ITC New Baskerville.

Not flying but falling . . .

—"ORPHEUS'S LAST LYRIC"

1

INTO THE AIR

The arena is almost dark, the crowd's frantic shrieks louder now, managed by light cues. I stand in the dimness at the side of the stage, holding hands with Joshua. Peering past him and the curtain, a spinning, giddy joy fills me again as I see them, hear them, feel them.

The crowd. Moving in the dark, waiting, screaming his name.

Joshua Blackbird.

"Is this real?" Joshua's voice is a low rumble. The skin under my ear tightens and pulls, almost as if wanting to yank my neck under his lips and press there.

I smile and steal a glance at him. In the dark his change-able hazel-green eyes are mostly pupil, fringed with lashes as dark as his shoulder-length hair, glossy as a raven's wing.

My voice is caught as I look at him. *Is this real?* I don't know anymore. They scream for this boy I've known my whole life. Now he's fifteen, nearly sixteen, and famous around the world.

I spot Ty, Joshua's little brother, in the front row. He's beaming pride, a thirteen-year-old trying to act older and cooler. His smile is a spotlight aimed at the stage.

Just eight months ago, we were all in tiny Marchant, Georgia. The only constant from then is the music. From the day I first met him, Joshua has always written songs. He used to lug around a thrift-shop guitar that was too big for him. He'd play for anyone who'd listen.

Now over twenty thousand people fill one of the most famous arenas in the world, waiting to hear him perform.

It's the opening night of his first tour.

"Band, go!" The stage manager's call launches more adrenaline into my veins.

The lights flick up and out, shooting across the arena before dimming. The massive screen above the stage starts to play footage of Joshua—behind the scenes, rehearsing, recording, all the while effortlessly smiling for the cameras.

As the band takes their places, silhouettes just visible to the crowd, a roar erupts. It's a sound I've never heard before.

Twenty thousand screaming fans, mostly girls, their desperate voices collectively piercing the air like a siren.

"Birdies," the female fans were dubbed by a blogger, and the name stuck.

Beside the stage, Joshua squeezes my hand before letting go. His hands come up and push back my razor-cut bright red hair. He kisses me, once.

Then he's gone. Onto the stage. Into their screams of love.

As Joshua moves onto the stage in the near dark, the pitch and timbre of the screaming increases. Joshua's hands rattle against his legs with nerves as Quinn, the lead guitarist, lifts the strap of Joshua's guitar and helps place it over his shoulder.

I still have to do a double take at the makeover transformation, remembering the Joshua of Marchant: the blunt haircut that Ty or I would give him, Joshua standing on the weathered wooden deck in front of their trailer as I snipped kitchen scissors in a nearly straight line along the tops of his shoulders.

Now his long hair is cut into layers and is perfectly tousled, and there's a stylist who travels with him to make sure it stays just so.

In Marchant he wore plain jeans and whatever cheap, wrinkled T-shirt he picked up off their shared bedroom floor.

Now he wears a sleek black-and-silver costume—tight pants with sneakers, a T-shirt, and a fitted jacket with accents on the back and arms that glint like dark chrome wing bones under the lights.

In Marchant he was my boyfriend. The boy next door who lived three trailers down from me.

Now he's everyone's imaginary boyfriend, an international star. It started with a handheld YouTube video that's been viewed over twenty-seven million times. His debut album, which came out just three months later, went double platinum, exploding like a rocket. "Number one with a bullet," his agent had said.

And here he is onstage, headlining his first tour.

In the near dark, you can feel the restlessness of the crowd. Expectation thrums in palpable waves. The glow of small screens, turned on and held up to thousands upon thousands of faces, aimed at the stage, each a pinpointed moment, a person, each a singular whole other world out there in the dark, twinkling together like a constellation.

"Cue sixteen. Lights ready!" the stage manager shouts into his headset.

"You did it, Shu," I say in a whisper. Onstage, Joshua turns to me as though he heard somehow and flashes me the smile I've known forever, the one that still makes my stomach clench with butterflies.

"Ready and go!" I hear behind me.

The stage lights flash on and sweep down, like the illumination of an angel descending.

I didn't think it was possible, but the cheering grows louder, crests like a wave, ricocheting around the cavern of the arena, searching for Joshua Blackbird.

The audience has one voice, and it crashes into us, a shriek of anticipation and desire.

The drummer, Speed, counts in with his drumsticks. Lights flash around him, backlighting the loose coils of his short Afro.

The drumbeat and a guitar start together.

The stage is awash with golden light, bright as an unending fall of stars. The scale of the room is unbelievable, the stage massive and yet swallowed by the space beyond it.

The distinctive chords of Joshua's first hit echo out, and the crowd starts bouncing—trying to dance in front of their seats, bodies and voices calling.

Joshua joins them, jumping in place easily, steadying his guitar with one hand, pumping his other arm in the air in time with the music.

Speed intensifies the beat, and then the familiar synth notes rise like bubbles, the hook in them so catchy I can't help but join in the dancing.

Even though I've heard this song a thousand times.

Dancers enter the stage, crossing the front, all silver flash and gyrations, forming a shifting shield in front of Joshua. They glide forward, keeping him nestled behind their bodies.

The immense screen over the stage both teases and reveals the object the Birdies all scream for as he moves closer to them.

Then the dancers part and Joshua steps to the edge of the stage. Hands reach for him, fingers hungry, camera phones glowing and devouring.

An enormous black-feathered bird crouches on the screen above. Then the raven lunges upward, opening ink-dark wings, a glare of light accentuating dark edges as it rises, wings sweeping wide.

And just like that, Joshua Blackbird takes flight.

2

SPINNING BEGINNING

eighteen months later

We've seen both oceans now, Joshua and me. He insisted for once, a year ago, when we were on the opposite side of the country in Atlantic City. It was right after he refused to see his father, even though the press heard his dad yelling as he was denied. Heard him yelling about all the ways he was going to make it right. How he was sorry he'd ever left. Asking why Joshua couldn't forgive.

On the way back to the hotel, Joshua had commandeered the car, insisting that we detour to the beachfront. We drove by the boardwalk, lit up like Christmas, and kept going until we found a quieter spot.

We held hands and pulled each other through the sand to the water's edge.

We were too tired to do anything but look at it,

standing on the battered sand, palms pressed together, staring out at the vast Atlantic Ocean, endless and indifferent and powerful.

Wave after wave, wearing the shore away by inches. Capable of eating holes into solid rock, depositing detritus on the shore, taking a part of what was there with each crashing arrival.

It was near the end of Joshua's first US tour, and it was all I could do to stand as the waves pulled solid footing from under my feet. It was one moment of peace in a frenetic ride that had taken over our lives.

Now it's time to start touring in support of Joshua's new album, *Flying Not Falling.* A full year this time, a world tour including Europe and Asia.

He's seventeen years old.

The opening night is tomorrow, here in LA. It's been sold out for months, and resale tickets online are at record-breaking highs.

Right now Joshua is finishing the last rehearsal at the arena, running light cues and costume changes, making the final adjustments before tomorrow night.

Around seventy journalists and photographers wait for him in this gilt-and-glass ballroom of the luxury hotel where we've all been living until the tour starts.

Joshua will arrive soon to answer their questions, like a prizefighter before the big match.

The past year and a half, and longer, has been a blur. It's like painting with smoke, trying to piece coherence together. Where we are. What came before.

What comes next.

Joshua's manager, Artie, works the room. She moves from journalist to journalist like a queen, slender and sharp as an ice pick, with a personality to match. She's impeccable, as always, wearing a dark suit and high heels, her face made up to perfection: mascara, blush, bloodred lips. Her bleached hair is woven into a braid, pulled over a shoulder. All-Business Rapunzel.

I don't bother with much makeup beyond eyeliner, preferably raccoon-smudged so it looks like I put it on yesterday and then slept in it.

I like it when my clothes don't fit or match, and it's best if everything looks like it was once a piece of something else. Like it was part of a uniform or a nice suit or simply belongs somewhere else, looking some other way. Like the clothes got lost or separated somehow, abandoned in a thrift store or found on the sale rack, and then maybe they went through hell trying to get back where they belonged, dinged up, torn, ripped, shredded. And I found them. And they belong with me now.

I rip them more and make them mine that way.

Artie glances at me. It's the same look every time. One part *oh God, her again*. And one part *what is she wearing?*

The only thing Artie and I have in common is that we match in stature and height. Slender and average respectively, with chemically treated hair. Although hers is supposed to look natural, unlike mine.

Bleach Blonde and Chemical Red. We should be superheroes saving Joshua.

We're not, but like superheroes, we spend a lot of time fighting each other.

Artie keeps moving through the ballroom, greeting her favorites among the waiting journalists. She likes her PR planned to perfection, and that can take careful massaging.

Artie had hoped the past weeks would be only about the buildup before the tour. The rigors of rehearsal, the growing artistry of her star. Even the devotion of the Birdies, or answering endless questions about Joshua's bubblegum pop girlfriend, Angel Rey.

I made a useful part of the story at first—the childhood sweetheart who followed Joshua Blackbird to the Big Time. Artie loved it once. She felt I made Joshua look authentic. Down-to-earth.

But the need for authenticity ended once Joshua's first album went double platinum. It was time to move on to something—and someone—more glamorous.

Angel Rey as Girlfriend is a publicity stunt that Artie dreamt up, manages, and uses. The fans of both stars devour every morsel of "news," not knowing that their on-again, off-again drama is completely manufactured.

I'm not his girlfriend anymore, officially. I'm now the "loyal friend" who sometimes causes Angel to feel jealous because of our history. Some teens identify with me, apparently. Most would rather be Angel Rey. Either way, the mill gets its grist.

The journalists call me "the girl from home" or "the other woman"—if I rate a mention at all. They say, "She'd be pretty enough if she smiled." Like there's a measurable scale of pretty that's allowable, and if I smiled, I'd tip over onto the "enough" side.

As if I'm ever going to smile just because someone told me it would make me pretty.

Artie walks past the journalists, a shark lording over barracudas. Each stiletto click of her heels is barely audible on the floor. I don't know how she does that, walks with near-predatory silence in heels over marble.

She climbs up the steps of the dais and moves behind a table covered with a white cloth. Several microphones are spaced evenly across the surface.

Artie takes a seat behind a microphone and turns a megawatt fake smile out to the audience of reporters.

"Joshua Blackbird is en route." She smiles bigger, a magician presenting a sudden bouquet. "He will take your questions. But"—she raises a red-lacquered nail—"all questions are to be limited to the topics of the new album and the upcoming tour. Or Angel Rey."

There is a collective groan from the reporters.

"Come on, Artie," someone calls out. "Everyone wants to know about the Boom Room—"

Artie leans over her mic, a bird of prey looming over a tiny, furred creature. Each word is a spike. "No. Questions. About. The club."

More murmurs of disgust. Someone yells, "That's why I'm here!" and someone else calls, "I got readers to feed!" sparking a round of derisive laughter.

"Artie!" a woman calls from the front row. "We love you, but this is a bunch of crap. You know we're here because of—"

"Let me be perfectly clear." Artie cuts her off as well. Artie's proven management technique: don't let the other person finish. "If anyone asks about the incident at the club, they will be frozen out from future press events. That's it. That's the deal."

Welcome to Artie's headache. Instead of the tour or the AngelBird romance, all anyone has wanted to talk about recently has been the Boom Room incident, which happened five days ago.

Even Artie's perfectly staged day at the beach for Joshua and Angel, all sunshine kisses and salt waves and perfectly mussed hair blowing in the breeze, wasn't enough to steer attention away from Joshua's two A.M. meltdown at an LA nightclub.

The paparazzi had been there, of course. They're camped outside anywhere Joshua goes, waiting for any sellable glimpse of America's boyfriend. They'd gotten more than their money's worth that night, even if no one is entirely sure how it went down inside.

The bandaged hand, the bloody lip. The strange, vacant look in Joshua's eyes as he slipped away from the handlers, his "entourage," and actually stood still for the cameras. Waiting for them to capture him.

But this is Artie's milieu. She cut her teeth on a press badge. And after having to manage what happened in Dallas last year, what happened at the Boom Room is simple enough. Not welcome, but easy enough.

The new normal.

"And now, before Joshua arrives, a special treat to reward your patience," Artie breathes into the mic, voice soft like she's speaking in church instead of in a hotel ballroom packed with journalists.

"The private premiere of Joshua's new single, 'Forever or Never,'" Artie says. "One-minute teaser." The speakers on the dais hiss and crackle, the manufactured sound of a vinyl record starting. Then a sampled loop of a woman singing three rising notes. A drumbeat and synthesizer start before Joshua's remarkable voice cuts in.

The assembled journalists wear one of three expressions: delight, professional boredom, disdain.

Do they realize we can read them as easily as they think they read him?

The song is going to be a massive hit. Anyone can hear that. It may even surpass his record-breaking single, "Armored Heart."

That was his breakout song. The moment everyone knew they were listening to a star.

Joshua wrote "Armored Heart" for me, sitting on the janky sofa in my grandma's trailer, strumming chords and jotting down lyrics. Trying to make me smile.

We don't talk about that. Artie told Joshua to stop telling that story.

The Birdies want to imagine he's singing to them. Or to Angel Rey, and never mind the time line. They want his voice intimate in their ears as they make fan art, or reblog fan works, or make GIFs. They watch the video over and over, and comment about it. A song that is for them now.

This new song, "Forever or Never," was written by committee. A perfectly orchestrated hit with that essential bit of "Joshua magic." The song of a lovestruck boy, promising an all-or-nothing devotion.

Joshua had winced when he saw how they'd changed his lyrics. "Vanilla trash," he'd called it.

Of course the changes remained. Artie handled that

situation as she does all situations: masterfully. Protecting Joshua's "brand" above all else.

I'd like to breathe fire at all of it. Ignite everything and let it be consumed. The fake girlfriend. The rehearsals, the interviews, the fan meet and greets, all of which wear him down. The individuals who wait for hours to smile for a picture, to hug him as they vibrate with emotion or tears, that make him feel more and more isolated by their wanting.

All of it.

I feel the sneer on my lips and turn away from the room, facing the mirrored wall. If someone were to take my picture, they'd use it to say I don't like the new song.

I press my forehead into the cool glass so I don't have to see how frayed I look.

Mere seconds later I feel someone standing next to me and open my eyes. In the mirror I see Artie reflected, standing behind me.

She takes my elbow and leans in close.

"Public face, sweetheart." Her voice is a low hiss by my ear. "Joshua needs you."

I try to pull away without looking like I'm doing it. I return her fake smile in the mirror.

"It's okay—he has you." Anger surfaces in my voice, a tiny bubble dredging up from a swamp, bursting at the surface. "And Angel."

Artie doesn't care about me. And I'm not convinced she really cares about him.

She smiles wider, refusing to take the bait. "Damn straight he has me. From the start."

Which is true. Artemis Malfa has managed Joshua Blackbird from the beginning. She nearly created him, showing up in Georgia with contracts and promises. She's fifteen years older than us but already a lifetime wiser.

She's the ringmaster. Her job is to keep everything going, no matter what it costs.

One night early in the first tour, maybe a month in, I didn't go to the arena. Angel Rey was going to be there, their first "date" since the tour started. It stuck in me like a poisoned dart, so I stayed in the hotel and watched TV instead.

There was a show on about the history of the circus. It was something I'd never thought of: how far it went back, how it had changed over the years. How circuses used to be *the* prime entertainment of the day.

Something about the combination of the old photos and film footage, and the idea of a circus as a living entity, a changing art form with a history full of people, trapeze artists and animal trainers, ringmasters and roughnecks, the people performing or the people watching, all trying to get away from their reality for a few hours. It just grabbed ahold of me.

I ordered a bunch of books and read more and more. I continually read and reread and think about it. Some of the people, long dead, are more fully real to me, more present, in the books and through how they lived their lives, than my mother ever was, even before she kicked me out.

I didn't realize at first how many parallels there would be—between the circus and the machine of *Joshua Blackbird*.

Now I'm mostly obsessed with a single person, Lillian Leitzel, a tragic aerialist from the twenties. I don't know why she fascinates me so much. I recognize something about her. And I guess I just need an escape.

Run away with the circus all you want. You can't outrun who you are or what you need.

Artie glares at me but turns back to the room as the new song ends. She smiles, touching her earpiece. No doubt listening to Santiago, Joshua's personal bodyguard.

Artie crosses in front of the journalists and stands at the emergency fire doors on the opposite end of the dais. When the double knock comes, she's ready.

Her voice is pitched to attract, a carnival barker reaching for marks.

"Ladies and gentlemen!" she shouts. "Joshua Blackbird!"

The chorus of "Armored Heart" blasts from the speakers on the dais.

Artie whirls and presses onto the crash bar hard, launching the door outward.

An explosive glare of daylight blinds us.

Two figures step in and immediately to the side of the door. These are Joshua's "friends from home"—two bros, Dan and Rick. They're from Marchant and were two grades above Joshua and me. When the first tour stopped in Atlanta, they finagled backstage passes and somehow never left.

Joshua sometimes hangs out with them, and Artie likes the story it tells. Joshua as "just one of the guys."

They're fake friends. A couple of clowns as boring and accommodating as furniture that blends with everything—they laugh when you crack a joke and ask nothing more than to sit on the periphery of it all.

The drummer, Speed, is the next through the door. He's handsome, with nearly poreless dark-brown skin and onyx eyes ringed by tightly curling lashes.

Everyone calls him "Speed" because he's always in motion—bouncing, rattling, drumming—like a hyperkinetic kid after drinking caffeinated cane syrup. He was the last musician to join Joshua's official band, "discovered" in an online video contest that Artie dreamt up.

He and Joshua became genuine friends almost immediately.

The rest of the band trots through the door: Quinn,

Stevie, and Jordy. They move onto the stage and wait at their seats.

A lithe figure moves into the sun's glare, delineated by the nearly impossible radiance outside. An inkblot against the light.

Then he's in the door and moving to the dais. The audience can't help but applaud.

His presence travels through the room, a heart-stopping frisson. Everyone holds their breath, watches, admires, in spite of their familiarity with his face and form, the inhabitants of this room a microcosm of the wider world and how everyone reacts to him.

Helpless in the thrall of Joshua Blackbird.

3

CONJURE A HOME

As Joshua enters, I hear the muffled shrieks of the Birdies who wait in the alley behind the ballroom.

It sets my teeth on edge.

Santiago, Joshua's bodyguard, is the last to enter. He closes the fire doors and then waits at the side of the dais. Arms crossed, he glares out at the room, eyes sweeping the front row of journalists, then checking the entrances, aisles, and edges of the room for threats.

The sight of him is immediately reassuring. Ever since Dallas, Santiago is a constant, looming presence in Joshua's periphery. He's an ex-marine, all bulk-corded muscle and vigilant eyes.

On the dais, Joshua pulls a chair out and sits. He takes

off his sunglasses and hunches behind the mic. His posture speaks for him.

He'd rather be anywhere else.

Even though his face is tipped down, the power of his presence is palpable. A moment, suspended in the air, sparkling as we watch the spotlights illuminate perfection.

And we respond with a held breath. A heart catch.

It's not just fame. It's not just his heartbreaking voice, startling good looks, or brooding, haunted eyes.

It's something more. Call it charisma.

As one, the room watches Joshua Blackbird, caught in an enchantment.

He's tall and lightly muscled with a handsome face, finely drawn features, like a portrait, or a high-fashion photograph, young masculine beauty almost inhuman, at times. Changeable hazel eyes, at this moment appearing green. High cheekbones, dark-winged eyebrows, and equally dark hair not an affectation, just a perfect punctuation of his last name.

Some fans are completely incapacitated by him.

Joshua tips his head to the side, looking for me. He spots me standing with my back pressed against a mirror in an inescapable room of reflections.

He looks so tired. Almost emptied out, like I'm seeing an echo of who he is in his eyes. Until he smiles at me, just a little.

For a moment, my heart is incapacitated as well.

A popping of flashes around the room, a strobe effect like being in a club, as the photographers capture the rare half smile.

As if a spell has been broken, journalists start shouting questions.

Joshua smiles at them professionally, shaking his head a little, like he is trying to wake up. His unstyled Mohawk falls in chopped layers over his eyes.

The close-shaved sides of his head are still startling. It makes him look simultaneously older and somehow more vulnerable.

The fans all cried at first, few weeks ago, when he shaved off his shoulder-length hair, leaving a short swath down the middle, floppy sometimes, Mohawk-spiked others. Some journalists called it rebellion, the evolution of the artist, rejection of his audience. Gossip bloggers called it a sign of mental imbalance or an act of continuing grief for his father. The result of strain and stress.

They were both right for a change.

As the shouted questions continue, Artie climbs onto the dais and holds up a hand. Then she points into the crowd.

The journalist, a young woman, calls out the first question.

"Feeling good about opening night tomorrow, Joshua?"

A softball, lobbed straight and slow, easy enough that a little kid could knock it out of the park.

"Great. It's going to be a great show. I have the best band and dancers. They make me look good."

Although it sounds a bit *aw shucks*, it's sincere, and comes across that way.

Even the borderline-hostile journalists nod at the perfect hit of the promotional target.

Artie continues pointing, faster and faster. The questions stay easy. She's picking and choosing her favorites to warm him up, like a trainer starting punching drills at a laughably easy level.

They ask about the album, the tour, the opening bands and guest performers, about Angel Rey: Will they do a duet soon?

Joshua answers each question well.

Artie's mouth tightens, and she points at another journalist, a man with the glint of razors in his eyes.

"What's your favorite part of the meet and greets?" he asks, smirking.

They all know Joshua tried to stop doing them. In the end, Artie convinced him they were necessary.

Joshua leans into the mic.

"The fans," he answers, clean sincerity again.

He sits back and smiles, and it hits them again as the flashes pop. As if he has just walked into the room for the first time.

Magic.

The smile that launched a thousand Tumblrs.

Most of the reporters smile back helplessly. Artie smiles, too, a scythe of satisfaction. She points again.

"Are your brother and mom coming to the show tomorrow?"

A simple question. A normal question.

Ty and Livie are in Georgia, living in the mansion Joshua bought for them.

Joshua's lingering smile slips. He glances down.

It's like a droplet of blood hitting the water. In their seats, the journalists still.

"I . . . I think there's something going on," Joshua stammers. "A school dance or something."

He looks younger. No, he looks his age. The surrealism of the situation hits me like an electric shock.

He shouldn't be here at all. This isn't normal.

"We'll see," Joshua concludes lamely. His fingers tap on the table. As he sits farther back, slumping down, a sliver of skin shows through a small tear on the chest of his dark T-shirt.

Another familiar sight. A memento from a fan's tearing hands.

Then I see it. Joshua's hand on the table trembles. It's subtle, like how a guitar string moves when it's plucked. An almost invisible, vibrating tension.

Joshua must have felt it, because he lifts his hand off the table, scowling.

Artie glares at the reporter, her red nails gripped tight on Joshua's shoulder. Her hand falls away as he pushes his chair back and stands.

He takes a step, moving into the arc of light cast down from a halogen bulb. His complexion takes on a sallow cast. The circles under his eyes jump out in contrast.

He's always been slender, but now he's tending toward too thin. Worn thin, like a fraying rope, rubbed raw with all our handling.

I push through a few of the crew and standing journalists, moving to the bottom of the steps, where Joshua can see me when he turns.

The other band members stand by their chairs and wait for Joshua to lead them off the dais.

It's like someone empties the room of all sound, except for the hum from the speakers.

"Joshua, are you okay?" a reporter, a man, calls. He looks like a TV dad. And I see how his question changes the perception subtly, as it ripples through the room.

Is Joshua okay?

I mean, on second thought, just look at him.

This time Artie doesn't answer for him or prod him for a response. She follows him to the steps and waits as he walks down them.

At the bottom, Joshua's hand brushes past mine. His is cold.

Santiago appears in front of us. The rest of his security team takes up formation, and we cross to the door that leads to the hotel elevators.

Artie returns to the stage and starts speaking into a mic, thanking the journalists for their time and offering to answer any additional questions they might have.

Joshua keeps his face tipped down as he walks, watching the heels of his bodyguard in front of us.

A single journalist pushes up and walks beside us to the doors. She paces our steps outside the bubble of security. Her voice is pitched conversationally, intimate as a friend.

"Joshua, are you homesick?"

He doesn't look at her when he answers.

"This is home."

We leave the ballroom, stepping into the cold elegance of the hotel hallway.

4

INNER WORKINGS

We step into the hallway and make it about five steps before the too-bright flare of a camera-mounted light glares in our faces.

"That was a short press conference," the guy yells as he's pushed back. "Not feeling it today, bro?"

I could learn his name if I wanted to know it. He's a lead reporter on one of those TV tabloid shows. The kind that features an assembly of "reporters" sitting around a "newsroom" sharing gossip, pronouncing judgment on everything.

Cutting knockoff fame from the whole cloth of actual celebrities.

Him and hundreds like him, the favored by Artie and the not-so-favored, are an omnipresent lens casting a mirror ball strobe of flashes. Reporting the rumors, the thinly veiled *guess who?* gossip items, endlessly picking at Joshua. At what happened in Dallas. Cutting at the wound. Reopening it.

It's always something. Before the Boom Room, it was the airport waitress, talking to the tabloid TV show about how Joshua wouldn't take a picture with her, how he pushed her, knocking a stack of dishes to the floor in the process. Which he did. The worst part of it, the cell phone video of him yelling, sounding unhinged. Crazed. Which he was, and yet it was rational in that moment, which they didn't show. Couldn't show . . . all the stacked pressures that led to that break.

Don't show the strain. Just show the dislocation. Then call him a spoiled brat. Or an entitled monster. Or if the tone is sympathetic, it's gaspingly so, full of gross devouring of his pain and receiving in return *the feels.*

Artie lies to us and maybe herself. She says it will be easier on the road. It's as if she's forgotten about how it really is: the slow drag of tired feet on a forced march.

The paparazzo presses forward and is shoved back again, less gently this time.

Santiago stands in front of us, watching his team perform its job to perfection. We move toward the elevator as it dings.

One of Santiago's security team is the last to board, moving his hands and his body to block as much of the photographer's shot as possible.

The doors close.

Silence reigns in the elevator, except for the classical music playing softly through the speakers.

At the top floor, the elevator doors open again.

We file into the hall, past the ornate gilded table and its profusion of exotic flowers, past a private receiving room and a gym behind glass, to the presidential suite.

The security guard on point steps aside as Santiago uses his key card to enter. We walk into the room as the team does a sweep. Santiago personally checks Joshua's bedroom.

Then the security detail exits. All except for Santiago, stationed by the door. As discreet as he can be while never leaving the room.

Joshua shuffles to the deep leather sofa and falls into it, propped in the corner, an orchestrated collapse. He's slouched low so his head is held up by the corner of the sofa.

He looks like he could fall asleep without moving anything but his eyelids.

"Rox." He speaks in little more than a whisper, resting his voice as much as possible. "Landing gear down. The albatross has landed."

He pats the sofa next to him.

He glances at me, and that little slippy, half-broken smile is there. Like he wants to crack another joke, but is too tired.

He still wants to make light for me.

I'd like to make light for him. Literally, to make light. Hold my hands cupped together and bring a ball of light, a tiny sun, glowing between them, sunlight spilling through my fingers, arcing out in healing warmth. I could open my hands, and the warm light could flit, like a small, gentle, straight-flying bird, into his chest. He'd sit up then. Sit up and smile like he used to do.

The one with no heartbreak in it.

But I can't conjure a sun. The most magic I have is to be able to smile back at him.

"Hey, Rox," he says, in that soft voice, like he has to comfort *me*. He lifts an arm, and I curl beside him, tucking in along his long frame.

He kisses the top of my head. I tilt my face, pressing my lips into the fabric on his chest. He touches my razor-roughed hair, smoothing it away from the edge of my face.

When I place my ear back against his shoulder, I can hear and feel the subtle workings of muscle, tendon, and joint as he pulls his fingers over my hair.

Aerialist Lillian Leitzel was famous for her dramatic planges. At the top of the circus tent, she would dangle from a single rope. Placing her wrist through a looped cuff, she would hang, and then start swinging. Her legs would lift, and her entire body would rise, up and over, up and over, her shoulder the axis point as she flipped. The audience would count each one, into the hundreds.

Each plange dislocated her shoulder, even as her ability to perform them made her a star. Even as each performance damaged her shoulder and her wrist, as the cuff cut into it night after night.

Joshua pulls his fingers over my hair as under my ear, his workings creak.

Three rapid knocks sound at the door.

Artie.

Santiago looks at Joshua. Joshua nods, and the door is opened.

Artie click-stab marches over to the sofa. She starts speaking without preamble.

"Next time try not to give *quite* the impression that you're running away. I've told you. It just makes it worse."

Joshua huffs air through his nose.

Artie smiles at him indulgently. Then she tilts her head and really looks at him. "Have you eaten?" She walks to the room phone.

"I'm not hungry," Joshua says.

"You have to eat."

After she finishes ordering, she's back in front of us.

The indulgence is gone, replaced by efficiency. Artie in manager mode.

"Okay. A few hours here. Eat, try to rest, relax. Then we'll go out to *The Late Late Show*."

Joshua heaves a monumental sigh. Under my ear, his heart beats steady and low.

"All the ramp-up stuff will be over soon," Artie continues, steamrolling his sigh. "And then it'll settle down on tour."

My voice cuts in before I decide to speak. "*Settle down?*" Incredulity comes across like I want a fight. "Do you even remember what touring is like?"

Joshua's hand drops and squeezes on my side. He doesn't want me to argue with her.

Joshua feels obligation like a sickness, and Artie knows it.

I squeeze him back, and it's only one part reassurance. The other part is *don't tell me to be quiet*.

Artie ignores me, focusing on Joshua. "I'm sorry we have to go through this part to get to the good stuff. But you're almost to the downhill slope."

I want to ask her what the good stuff is.

Is it the press conferences? The performances? A barrage of questions shouted at you as you're blinded by flashes simply trying to get to a car?

Or is it writing songs that have half the lyrics, the

best, most human ones, changed by a committee devoted to manufacturing hits? Songs that lack soul, but hey, you can dance to them.

Artie stands up straight and pulls the braid over her shoulder. Smooths it there, like an ice princess confident in her powers.

Let it go.

"When the food gets here, I need you to eat. You have to keep your energy up."

The tone. The mother tone. The one I can't stand.

The one that pulls every one of Joshua's strings. Jerks him upright and gets him going. Can get him walking on a hairline fracture, or singing with strep.

Or performing again, two weeks after Dallas.

I can feel it in his posture. In the grip that loosens around my ribs.

Acquiescence. Ms. Kearney, our teacher, would have called it that. She would have taught it to us, wanting us to learn the name of something we already knew by heart.

A big word that means surrendering another part of yourself.

That was back when we still did schoolwork. Back when Joshua and I had lessons on the bus, or in a corner of a studio somewhere. When we all thought he and I would graduate high school.

That was then.

It wasn't that long ago that it stopped, only two months. But it feels like a lifetime now. So many different things happened at once when Joshua turned seventeen.

He got emancipated completely and dropped out of school. Artie let Ms. Kearney go. I finished my semester out doing schoolwork online.

It's summer now, but I'll drop out too, in the fall, when I turn seventeen.

With Joshua it all happened in a breathtaking series of pen slashes—signatures across papers. A coming of age that wouldn't ever be shown in a corny montage in a movie.

But once he was emancipated, he didn't need Artie to act as his legal guardian anymore. Or Livie to act as his bank. He could control his own money.

Which, strangely, he started throwing away. He went on a spree that still hasn't stopped. He bought houses for everyone. Starting with my grandma—a nice, one-level house in a privately patrolled neighborhood.

He wouldn't listen to me argue why he shouldn't spend like that.

He reminded me what happened the last time we were photographed kissing. A certain type of fan went after me. Hordes of them. Online, spewing hate. Then I got doxed. My old address and phone number got sent out online.

Grandma called me in tears from the harassment. I helped her move into an apartment.

Then Joshua bought the house.

He didn't stop there. He met with a lawyer, an accountant, a tax specialist. He set up a series of accounts, gifted some to us. Me, his mom, his brother.

He bought an astonishing amount of property: land, houses, condos, a villa in France, a beachside retreat in Mexico, a Putt-Putt amusement complex near our hometown. He bought them all.

And then he gave them away. Or most of them, at least.

He gave houses or land or office suites to all of us, the ones closest to him. I don't even know how much he's kept for himself. Not much. There's a mansion in LA he bought but hasn't set foot in. And the beach house in Mexico he bought without seeing, just watched a video online and showed it to me, this modest white stucco cottage overlooking the Pacific.

We haven't set foot in that one, either.

I've lost track of it all. If he sees something, he gets it. Then he gives it away. Property, cars, music equipment and instruments, and expensive gadgets. Drones, clothes, shoes, entertainment systems, books, tablets, TVs, hover boards, go-karts, pool tables.

He doesn't keep much of anything.

Artie is still looking at Joshua, unsatisfied with his nod. "Do you need me to call Dr. Matt?"

Our teacher has been let go, but Joshua's personal doctor is still on the payroll. It's not like the medicine he dispenses to Joshua is unnecessary. Lots of high achievers have focus problems. Or need help resting. Or need help mustering extra energy. Or need help to get through whatever moment faces them.

Dr. Meadows gave it to me, Rox. Don't look at me like that. Just to take the edge off.

The edge that is always there.

It's something else we try not to fight about.

"I'm fine," Joshua whispers to Artie. "I just need to be quiet for a bit."

So we sit in relative silence. The air-conditioning clicks on and off. Maybe Joshua even falls into a light doze. I certainly do, with my head cradled on his shoulder, listening to the gentle drum of his heart.

I wake up when Artie directs the food to be placed on the coffee table in front of us. I blink, trying to think what I ordered, then remember Artie ordered for us.

There's too much food. An assortment of sandwiches and salads. There's at least three different varieties of thin broth, a fail-safe food for Joshua.

Teas and sodas and coffee and designer water.

My stomach growls, and I sit up. Behind me, Joshua laughs, a low rumble.

I turn to look at him.

He points to his shoulder where my head recently rested. A damp patch darkens his shirt.

"Guess you were really out, huh?" he whispers.

"Shut up." I can't help smiling at him. I wipe my cheek off.

"Sleeping Drooly."

"Keep it up, Blackbird."

"Oh, yeah? Or what?" He forgets and speaks at his normal volume.

"I'll start reading Birdie fanfics. Out loud."

Joshua holds up his hands, laughing a little. "Anything but that!"

I grab a plate with a club sandwich and chips and start eating. Beside me Joshua sits up. He looks at the food, then looks away.

Artie notices and marches over from the periphery of the room. "Eat something, Joshua," she orders.

Joshua gives her a look, but he grabs a mug of broth and sips it.

Artie sighs.

"I wish you had Rox's appetite."

I feel myself sitting hunched over the plate like someone is going to fight me for it. Unable, even after all this time, to relax when I'm actually hungry. Unable to accept that the food is going to be there again when I want it.

Like me, Joshua still keeps food stashed in his pockets, protein bars or fruit grabbed off the catering table in the rehearsal hall. Even if he doesn't eat them.

Old habits.

Artie's words are a dig. Like how she looks at my clothes or hair or combat boots.

I stay curled over the plate. Tilt my head up at her and take a massive, nearly choking bite of the sandwich. Scatter a piece of lettuce and a bit of meat.

Then I add a smile.

Artie glares at me, shaking her head. But she doesn't say anything else.

And I leave it at that, because Joshua didn't notice. And to tell the truth, I wish he had my appetite, too.

Any appetite.

I finish my food, and Joshua has more broth, and then it's time to get ready for his performance on *The Late Late Show.*

Joshua hates TV shows, hates backstage, hates the greenrooms, so he waits as long as he can in the hotel and gets ready here.

DeeDee the stylist arrives, pulling along a wheeled cart with plastic-sheathed wardrobe choices. A makeup holster is strapped low across her hips.

"I don't need to change," Joshua says. He slumps back in the sofa, head propped in the corner.

DeeDee doesn't say anything. She simply looks at Artie.

"Your shirt is ripped. Change that at least." Artie crosses her arms across her stomach. All perfectly placed talons and sharp elbows.

Joshua leans forward and scrubs his face with his hands.

He used to argue with Artie about everything. Big things, little things. Stupid things, just to get her worked up.

Now he never contradicts her.

I don't know when he stopped, and it bothers me that such a fundamental change crept up on me.

Joshua stands and walks over to DeeDee. He pulls a hanger off the rack. A new shirt, identical to the torn one. He turns away from us before pulling the torn shirt off over his head. Even though we've seen the slight, jagged scar across his abdomen numerous times. Even though it's been photographed for official court records. Even though some of the photos got leaked and it was splashed across tabloids and gossip blogs.

He still turns away.

Artie waits until he turns back around and then crosses to Joshua.

"Let me look at you."

He looks down into her face. She smiles approval and squeezes a rare hug into him. More mothering. Joshua leans into it, bending low to return the hug below her uplifted arms. Artie's arms are tight across his shoulders as a hand pat-pats. A *this hug is ending soon* gesture.

She lets go before he does, then leans away.

Joshua's arms drop.

"Let me just . . . " Her voice trails off as she picks up an eye pencil and retraces his startling eyes.

He stands as she does it, perfect as a statue. Expression neutral, the shape of his closed mouth, lips full but not lush, hinted smile-curves at the corners, now held flat as he watches her, waiting for her to finish with him.

Sometimes looking at Joshua is like falling endlessly, knowing it's happening, unable to stop yourself.

Artie puts the eye pencil down. DeeDee steps in and fluffs and spritzes Joshua's floppy Mohawk. After a moment, she nods and steps back.

"Let's go," Joshua says.

He takes my hand and squeezes like he's slipping into ice-cold water.

5

THE CLAWS OF BIRDS

The ride to the studio is quick and uneventful, then we're through security onto the studio lot, and arriving at the backstage door.

I walk with Joshua, with Artie behind us, through the crowd of waiting greeters and crew.

I feel their eyes on me as I walk with him, and the growl curls in my stomach, an anger I can't express. Because I can't hold his hand. Can't squeeze it gently, sending him strength. Can't prompt him to look at me. Because we are in public, and I'm not his official girlfriend.

We walk to the privacy of the greenroom, where we'll only wait a few moments.

Once inside, Joshua takes my hand. His smile is somehow . . . sad.

"Thanks, Rox," Joshua says. "I know you don't like this part."

As if there were any part left that I do like.

"It's okay, Shu," I say, the old nickname from back home.

"Rox." There's that sad smile again.

I dart a quick kiss on his cheek.

"Shu."

The rock in his shoe.

While we wait, a nervous production assistant hovers nearby, rattling off an unnecessary list of instructions. Joshua ignores the PA and the table of food and drinks. At the bar, Stevie, the bassist, mixes himself something dark and strong and downs it in one go.

The PA puts her hand to her ear, then stands and moves to Joshua's elbow.

"Okay, they're ready," she says.

It's not a long way to the studio stage. We push though fire doors, then stage doors. Although we can't see the audience on the other side of the curtain, their cheers are overpowering.

The house band plays out to a commercial break.

Speed nods at me, twirling a drumstick in his long fingers. The stage lights silhouette his floppy Afro as he walks over to join us.

He clasps Joshua's hand and gives him a one-armed

hug. Speed knows better than any of the others how depleted Joshua is right now. Speed's been there, talking to Joshua and me, or listening, or just quietly showing care with light touches on my head or Joshua's shoulders, a presence like a scaffolding, holding us up.

Speed frowns and steps close to me, tucking his drumsticks in his back pocket. I take his hand, lacing my fingers through his, pale through dark, like a negative exposure each of the other, meshed in the backstage gloom.

He turns and takes Joshua's hand.

The three of us stand linked: Joshua, Speed, and me. A fragile chain.

"Okay." Joshua takes a deep breath.

Speed squeezes my hand and lets go of both it and Joshua's at the same time.

A crew member gives Joshua a guitar. Joshua holds the guitar loosely by the neck as the other band members huddle in.

I step back.

Santiago moves to the edge of the yellow-taped visibility line, standing behind the curtain out of sight from the cameras. He scans the front row of the theater, the aisles, the exits.

Artie smooths her bleached braid and adjusts her shirt, as if she will be taking the stage instead of her client.

Joshua and his band walk out onto the stage as the host announces them.

The director has allotted a few extra precious seconds to allow for all the screaming. Then the band rocks into the new single, "Forever or Never."

Joshua sings and plays perfectly. More than perfectly. He's transformed, smiling, making eye contact with the camera. It even looks like he's having fun.

When the song ends, the Birdie-packed crowd screams fit to shatter glass. The host can barely make his sign-off heard.

Then it happens. A fan rushes onto the stage from the front row. It's a young woman wearing a T-shirt emblazoned with Joshua's face.

She pushes through the band, buffeting past the host, who lets out a startled "whoa!" She grabs on to Joshua, hanging off his neck, dragging on him with a hug that is half tackle.

My hands are balled-up fists, in my head a thunder-clap of anger and the buzzing fear-dump of adrenaline.

Santiago moves onto the stage instantly and crosses to Joshua. He takes the fan's arm and lifts, pulling her off him.

Another fan runs forward. Then another. Then ten more, a rush like the tide.

The house band stops playing.

I hear Santiago shouting. More security converge on

the stage. It's too little, too late as the entire first three rows rush at us.

Joshua turns toward me and bolts, half lunging, half shoved by Santiago toward the exit a few paces from where I stand.

Two more security members of Santiago's team join in, attempting to cover Joshua.

As they get nearer to me, the fans arrive as well, buffeting. Pushing and cheering. Some of them start grabbing anyone they find, hugging strangers, crying or throwing their arms into the air in celebration of their audacity.

I can't see Joshua. Or Santiago.

"It's *her*! *It's Roxy*!" a high-pitched voice shrieks by my ear, and I'm engulfed in a terrifying instant of fame by association.

Arms grab at me, and phones are pressed in my face. A tear on the neck of my T-shirt widens as I am grappled into hugs I don't want.

More voices join in as more people arrive—a bottle-neck at the exit, and I am trapped against the wall.

I shove out, hard. Panic crests in my chest, and I start punching wildly. My steel-toed Doc connects with a shin, and a girl yelps, turning eyes wide with betrayal at me.

I want to maim her. All of them.

Instead I take a deep breath. "I'm sorry," I blurt out as we are buffeted from all sides.

"Clear the building!" a voice shouts over the speakers "Anyone remaining in the studio when the police arrive will be arrested. Clear the building."

There is instant relief as those nearest the main doors leave. Then Santiago is there beside me, forcing people back and boosting me toward the stage door.

We barrel through the hall, past the greenroom, out into the alley.

More fans scream and press against the metal barriers.

Santiago and I jump into the SUV, and it pulls away.

Artie is disheveled. Her shirt is untucked, and her hair is mussed as if it, too, was grabbed.

Joshua curls against the opposite car door, his eyes wide as he watches me try not to shake.

We ride in silence.

The phone in Artie's hand rings. She listens, then hangs up.

Her face is a storm.

"It's already out. Cell phone footage and the show, too," she says to the entire car. Then she looks at Joshua. "Stay offline. You too, Roxanne."

I sink down into the seat. What if there's footage of

me kicking and punching? It will look bad, regardless of what was really happening. Or how scared I was.

I tell myself that it was too crowded. That even with the cell phones out, once it started, there's no way anyone could have seen me, how I reacted.

But if I'm wrong . . .

I'll be dragged online again. Worse than last time. But at least this time Grandma will be left out of it. Fringe benefit to Joshua's largesse and his home-buying spree.

No one knows where she is now. So I won't be doxed, and she won't be pestered by angry fans because of me.

"You know I never go online." Joshua's voice sounds wrung out. "Santiago carries my phone. He posts for me. Or Speed does."

"I know. Keep it that way," Artie says, and doesn't bother with me.

I have an old-fashioned flip phone. I only text Joshua, Grandma, and sometimes Speed, and I never, ever go online.

It's not a healthy place to be. For me. Anymore.

Artie texts on her phone, lighting quick.

"The studio head has our back," she says. "I'll get a team on any individual complaints that arise. The footage so far is fine."

She smooths her hair as we arrive at the hotel.

"We'll go up to the suite. I'll have a quick interview scheduled with *Entertainment Today*. That will cover it."

Joshua just nods.

Artie takes a deep breath. Then it appears, the gleaming smile. "You can't buy better press."

I want to laugh. Or cry.

Or kick someone else.

6

LOST ONES

After the *Late Late Show* performance, Joshua waited in a separate hotel suite for the damage-control interview with *Entertainment Today*. Then he remained there for another hour for a surprise VIP meet and greet that Artie couldn't turn down, A-listers who saw the *Late Late Show* performance and wanted to commiserate.

Joshua slid into and out of performance, *Joshua Blackbird* like a shell, or a skin that he could take off. Yet every time it comes off, it seems to take a piece of him with it, selfhood a slowly lost battle, a quiet erosion.

A war of attrition. Ms. Kearney would be happy I remember that phrase. A battlefield term for the bloodless fight that whittles you away.

When it's done at last, we ride up to Joshua's suite on the top floor to settle in for the night.

Joshua separates from the rest of us in the sitting room. He disappears into the bedroom, leaving the door only slightly open.

He's on the phone, sitting in an overstuffed chair by the window. I wait at the bedroom door until he nods at me. Then I collapse across his bed with my book.

Speed hangs out in the sitting room watching TV with the guys from Marchant, Dan and Rick.

When I met him, Joshua was a skinny boy with a kid brother, and Dan and Rick weren't our friends.

Before he got famous. When I was little, before I went to live with my grandma for good, when I'd just be visiting, I'd see Joshua around the trailer park. The first time we met, he was seven, I was six, and his brother, Tyler, was five.

Joshua tried to be nice to me. I kicked him in the shin for it.

We didn't talk again for years. I didn't really even feel bad about it, or think about it, until I moved in with Grandma when I was fourteen and saw him again.

We were in the same English class. Even though he's a year older than me, we were both in the ninth grade because Livie had made him stay home an extra year to take care of Ty. That way they could start school at the same time, Ty in kindergarten, Joshua in first grade. By skipping kindergarten and staying home that extra year, Joshua let Livie work and not have to pay for day care for Ty.

Helpless and apathetic as a parent, she at least knew enough not to leave a four-year-old alone with their dad, who, before he left for good, never did much beyond sit in front of the TV and drink.

On my first day in ninth-grade English class, I was so angry and was pretending I wasn't. I had only moved in with Grandma for good the previous week. Joshua walked into the classroom, and I knew he was the kid I had kicked all those years ago. And I thought, *Great. Just great.*

But he smiled at me.

Later he said he liked my hair, how it looked like it had been cut with a knife and was so red it looked like it was on fire. He wasn't intimidated by my combat boots or my black jeans with the knees torn out. Or how I tended to glare at everyone.

That first day, there had been a ring of empty desks around me.

Joshua sat right next to me.

Even back then, he was beautiful. It was a little hard to think of anything to say when I actually looked at him. And I did like looking at him. It was obvious, to me at least, that most of the other girls in class and some of the boys did, too.

Joshua seemed oblivious to the admiration.

He sat and started talking, first just talking, but then the questions came. *Where did you move from? What kind of music do you like? Do you like living at Avalon Estates? Isn't that the dumbest name for a trailer park?*

By the end of class, I'd decided he was okay. Maybe more than okay.

At the end of the day, we rode the same bus home together, sitting on the same bench, Ty sitting across the aisle.

Grandma liked him, said he was a good kid. That was high praise from her, so I knew it was true. Grandma has a compass for a heart, always pointing true north. Her eyesight was already so bad she could barely drive anymore, but she could see into people like they were made of clear glass.

Though I think the real reason she liked him was that he recognized the Johnny Cash song playing on her radio. I never really listened to what Grandma played; to me it was all background, even as she hummed along. But Joshua knew all the words to "Folsom Prison Blues" and lit up around Grandma and her music. Gospel, country, bluegrass—he loved it all. When Joshua was around, Grandma turned up her music loud, leaning forward in her chair like she was about to get up and dance. Sometimes Joshua would sing along to the radio and Grandma would just take in the show and smile.

Joshua and Ty spent a lot of time at our house. Our circumstances were different, but only superficially so, like the insides of the trailers themselves. A little different, mostly the same.

A similarity: there was never enough money. A difference: Joshua didn't like that I shoplifted, and I didn't like that he didn't. I never took anything I didn't need.

He never took anything he did.

But we found our ways around each other's fault lines. Became friends. Then more than friends. Love like learning, actually learning, who you are and who the other person is. Who you want to be, and being that person, your true self, with someone who recognizes you. And loves the person you are, and the person you can be, and the person you are not—when you fail.

Love is like a tangle. A thorny vine surrounding something precious. But people think of it as magical, like watching an acrobat, suspended in the light, shining like a diamond. It looks effortless.

But it's not.

Now we're in a hotel, on the other side of the country from where we started, and things are so much harder, even if there's always enough money. In spite of how hard Joshua throws it all away, with both hands, ever since he turned seventeen. Like he can't get rid of his money fast enough.

Dan and Rick laugh at something on TV, raucous crows calling.

I turn the page of my circus history book, skimming for more information on Lillian Leitzel. She was the first performer in the history of the circus to demand and receive her own private carriage on the train.

Imagine, knowing your worth like that.

I keep reading about all the parties in the roaring twenties, how Henry Ford wooed her, waited for her at her railcar, filled it with flowers. And how a Chicago magnate proposed marriage. Threw a massive party for her, gave her a diamond tiara, all for the wild abandon of her aerial performances.

But the love of her life was the trapeze star Alfredo Codona, although in the end their love became yet another tragedy. But at first, they were magical: the King of the Trapeze and the Queen of the Air. Alfredo always envisioned himself Leitzel's romantic guardian. He would dress as a roustabout and check her rigging himself, every performance. Or he would dress in stagehand's clothes and act as her spotter as she flipped and twirled.

Joshua has been on the phone nonstop. First talking to Artie. Then to Speed in his own room one floor down, before Speed cut out the technological middleman and just came up, hanging out in real life. Then Joshua called Quinn, the lead guitarist. It's strange, in a way, the time he's spending on the phone with those who are closest to him now. It's like he's catching up after a long absence.

When we're all right here for him and will be here on tour with him for the next year.

But everything's strange now. And maybe this is healthy, Joshua taking this time to decompress and connect with those around him. When it has nothing to do with a performance.

I listen closely to his murmurings. Speaking softly to rest his vocal cords.

"Mom, please. Is Ty awake?"

My heart stills and falls.

He's talking to Livie.

Joshua stands at the windows beside the overstuffed chair where he'd been sitting before this moment. Before this call.

"It's not that late," he says, after listening briefly.

He doesn't need to be talking to her, not now.

"No, it's not," Joshua says. His hand tugs at his hair, pulling it back, a quick gesture of impatience and frustration.

I've heard it all before. I've been in the room between them, on the phone or in person, so many times that I can guess exactly her end of the conversation, murmured into his ear.

Ty used to come visit, short bursts, a weekend or a part of a weekend. Now he never comes, even though he wants to. He loves everything about his brother, even the rock-star lifestyle.

Especially the rock-star lifestyle.

But Livie keeps him in Georgia with her, in the mansion Joshua bought for them. Ty attends a private school, which is funny in its own way, because Ty is a lackadaisical student at best, unconcerned in subjects where Joshua was fascinated. Ty is mostly interested in engines he can take apart with his hands. Lawn mowers, mopeds, and finally his greatest love: dirt bikes.

And his idol, his big brother. Ty's eyes light up when he sees him.

If Ty had his way, he'd spend his days in the shop or on the track, or he'd stay with us, and not at the fancy private school where the kids all wear uniforms. But Livie insisted.

Joshua pays the tuition.

Livie puts up walls between Joshua and Tyler now, or tries to. I can't say I don't understand it, a little. At the same time, it's unfair. It's reasonable and unfair.

Livie likes to pretend she's aggrieved. Like a Greek tragedy somehow, nothing is ever her fault and she's always been wronged. So she pretends that keeping Ty away from Joshua is something she does out of protectiveness and wanting "what's best for him," but really it's all about leverage—ever since Joshua got emancipated.

"Quit stalling and put him on." Joshua knocks the filmy curtain aside and presses a fist on the glass door to the balcony.

I can imagine Livie's response.

No, he's asleep.

"Wake him up, then." Joshua presses his forehead to the cooling glass, next to his fist.

I won't. You shouldn't call so late, anyway. I was asleep.

"I'm sorry I woke you up, but I really need to talk to him."

You can talk to me. What's up?

Joshua bangs his forehead against the glass, once, quick, then drapes the fist over his head, forearm pressing into the glass, like he could release the tension, could warp the glass he leans on, curling and shimmering from the heat of internal pressure.

"I can't talk to you."

Are you trying to hurt my feelings?

"No, it's just the truth."

You don't even try.

"You don't listen."

And now I wish I could slip out without him noticing me. Because the intimacy feels like too much, even though I know he hasn't forgotten I'm here.

This time Livie takes the conversational ball and runs with it, and Joshua stands listening, a taut wire of tension, pressed against the glass.

I don't know what she's saying, but I can guess.

It's a song that's new but already sounds familiar, from

the first verse, something you've heard before and can almost hum along to.

Things like *That's a horrible thing to say.* And *All I ever wanted was what you wanted.* Or *All I ever did was support you.*

She'll build it up, a master manipulator. She'll start with her feelings being hurt, then she'll switch to being protective. *Who should I talk to? Do you want me to fire Artie? I'll do it!* A false ferocity that everyone but Joshua can see through.

I guess to him, it feels like love. Like Mama Bear's protection, the things he wants and never ever gets. Never had.

Mama Bear was the one who sold her cub to the circus.

After faking protective instinct, she'll switch to sympathy and coaxing. The *I know you're tired but* phase. Or the *I know you're scared but* phase, which started after Dallas. The endless reasons he can't ever stop. It's too late now. Everyone's depending on him, not her certainly, but the crew, the managers, the musicians, the label, everyone who ever did anything for him, like he *owes them,* when it was only ever just business. When they owe so much to him.

She'll make it an obligation, a tie of blood, something that becomes a yoke around his neck.

Indentured servitude he can never work off. And if he had any stamina, he'd see it will all get better. He just has to tough it out.

This time, Joshua cuts her off.

"Fine," he says. "Let him sleep. But tell me about him. Is he happy? What have you guys been up to?"

His voice and his question, the one behind the words, asking one thing: *Tell me about home.*

The one he bought them.

He eventually uncurls from the glass door, sitting back in the deep chair nearby, leaning into the phone as she talks.

Occasionally he says little things like "Yeah?" and "That was stupid." And I imagine her, weaving him stories about Tyler, what he's up to, what he said yesterday.

They talk about Tyler's date to the upcoming school dance, what she's like, and where Tyler is going to take her for dinner beforehand.

And who knows if any of it's even true?

Then Joshua laughs, a little polite sound, nothing behind it, just an echo of hers as she finishes another funny Tyler story.

And then he's silent. Sprawled in the chair, phone to his ear.

Annoyance gathers in my chest like a curl of smoke rising over dry leaves. Something that could become a blaze and consume me if I let it.

Because I know what she's doing now, too.

She's telling Joshua about the repairs to the roof. Or about how the pool has a leak. Maybe she's telling him about how his dog needs another surgery, or about how Tyler's dentist said he should have his wisdom teeth out. That the car is making a funny sound. A myriad of things that amount to *send money*.

There's always something, and she always asks, never waits for another time, always asks, every time they speak, every time he calls her or she calls him.

Livie never seems to have enough money.

Even though after he got emancipated, he bought her a house and a car and an RV and a fancy high-rise condo at the beach. Even though he gives her a monthly allowance. Even though she could easily make her own way if she just *tried*.

Joshua will listen, and he'll give it to her, whatever she asks for. He'll say, "Okay." He might even smile, like he used to at first, when he was happy to give. When it didn't feel like the only thing she ever wanted from him.

But Joshua doesn't say anything. The hand not holding the phone is gripped tight, fingers digging into the cushioned armrest like a claw.

"Jesus. Stop, Mom," Joshua says. "Just stop."

My heart jumps at the change to the script. The fact that that he's reached a limit.

"I'll send you the money. Of course I will. Stop telling me why you need it. I don't care why. You can just have it."

He's silent again. And I don't know what she could be

saying now, because this is a new conversation, him telling her to stop.

Joshua sits up suddenly, leaning forward in his chair. "I thought you said he was asleep."

Tyler.

"Hell, yeah, put him on!"

Livie—waking up Joshua's kid brother, a deflection. A scramble to consolidate her position—perhaps feeling precarious that Joshua just told her off, quietly but definitively. Afraid she's pushed him too far.

"Tyler! How you doing, little brother?"

I can hear a faded smile in Joshua's voice.

"You were asleep? Sorry—I really needed to talk to you."

Listening.

I can picture Tyler—floppy blond hair falling into the same changeable hazel eyes as Joshua. But his eyes don't brood, and he always wears an openhearted smile that comes from his and Joshua's father, from when he was younger. You can see it in the only picture of him that Livie displays, the two of them at a high school dance, flowers on her wrist as they smile in front of a balloon arch. Ty's already taller than me, tall like his brother, but I always think of him as a little pest, always tagging along.

Joshua gets up and walks to the window again.

He looks out into the darkness, listening to his brother

over long distance. "Yeah, I wish you could come out here, too. It's been a while since I seen you."

The slightest edge of Joshua's accent creeps back into his voice when he talks to Ty. Only Ty. Something about talking to his little brother transports Joshua back to Marchant, to who he was before.

Joshua listens, and the wistful smile returns.

"Yeah, thanks. It's going to be fine. You listen to me: don't worry about it. Have fun being a kid. Have fun at that dance. Treat that girl proper."

Then he laughs at something Ty says.

"Mostly proper, then."

Then he's pinching his eyes, like he has a headache, or is trying not to cry.

"I love you, too." Joshua turns and looks at me. "Hey, Rox wants to talk to you." He crosses to the bed. "Listen, I'm going to go. I got people waiting for me—but you have fun at the dance, okay?"

Then without giving Tyler a chance to respond, he shoves the phone into my hand and walks out of the room, going to join the guys watching TV.

Speed and Dan and Rick. None of them the person he really wants to see. Just the ones who are there.

"Ty," I say into the phone.

"Hey, Rox." Tyler's voice is sleep-croaky. "Is everything okay? Joshua sounds weird."

"I don't know." It's the truth. "He's under a lot of pressure."

Also true.

"Yeah, but that's nothing new."

I sigh and lean back against the headboard. "It adds up." Thinking about pressure, how it changes you. How it's changed him. The way that pressure accumulates, stacking down on you. "It's not always so fun being THE Joshua Blackbird . . . you know?"

Pressure creates diamonds. I read that on a poster once.

True enough. Pressure also warps steel.

Pressure creates an earthquake.

"Well, it's cool you're there for him," Tyler says. "He's lucky."

Is he? I think how empty Joshua looks. How tired we both are.

"Hey, Roxy, are you . . . are you crying?" Tyler's voice cracks, that pubescent squawk.

God, he's such a kid.

"Ty, tell your mom, tell her she has to stop asking for money every damn time he calls. Okay? And tell her to call *him* for a change. Do it, Tyler."

"Okay, Roxy."

"And you should come out. Bring your date. Wouldn't that be better than a dance? Just bring her to the show."

"I'd love to be there, but I'm not bringing a date to

my brother's concert. Not only is it gross, but if I even got to first base, I'd always wonder."

"Wonder what?"

"If she really liked me. You know. *Me.*"

I can't help the laugh. "You already wonder that. It's not like people don't know who your brother is."

"Right." He laughs too. "Well, I don't want to be that guy."

You're so not that guy, I think.

"Good point," I say. "Good to stay vigilant against that guy as much as you can. Given the circumstances."

Ty laughs. Then there's an empty moment, a hiss of silence.

"I guess I should go," Ty says at last. "Take care of yourself."

"I will," I answer. "You too."

We'll all do our best to take care.

7

AERIALIST

After I get off the phone, I go to the bedroom door and look out into the sitting room—see Dan and Rick, these guys I barely even know, lying collapsed, airless bags of skin and bone, watching the TV.

Speed is sitting off to the side, watching Joshua more than the TV.

Joshua sits outside on the balcony, visible through the mostly closed sliding glass door. He sits on the concrete, one long leg propped up, the other sprawled straight as he works on something before him.

I walk silently over thick carpet to the balcony. Pull the door open and semiclosed again behind me.

Joshua glances up for only a moment, then bends back down over his project.

I sit next to him, feeling the cool of the concrete through the heavy fabric of my army fatigues.

A small stack of papers sits on the balcony floor in front of Joshua. He's rotating and folding a page, turning, pressing a line, folding, pressing another line, reversing the fold.

Paper airplanes.

"You need sleep, Shu," I say.

He darts a glance at me. "Not tired." He picks up the paper plane, adjusts the wing flaps.

"This is my third design. Remember making these? We'd watch those YouTube videos?"

He pops up on his knees and hobbles over to the railing.

It's late. Nineteen floors below us, the pool is closed. The bar is closed, but the lights twinkle on, illuminated artificial warmth, a staged scene of all the luxuries that await.

The lighted past, tracer trails of all the fun you had.

Joshua takes aim and lets the airplane sail out into the night. It spins slowly, giant spiral loops as it falls and finally lands in the pool below.

Another paper airplane is already taking on water in the pool, waterlogged wings unfurling, paper resigning itself to water.

The third airplane lies on the pool deck, a perfect landing.

I reach over and grab several pieces of paper. We sit

in silence for a long time making airplanes, taking turns throwing them out into the cold night air.

"Remember this one?" I say at last, holding up a paper cylinder with a double-folded front edge.

Joshua smiles, and it lifts something in me, like paper caught on a breeze.

"Yes!" he says, and stands. He takes my hand and pulls me up.

"It's the best flier," I say, holding it with my thumb and fingers spread into a wide cradle. "You wouldn't think so, but it's the best."

"Not an arrow. A cylinder," Joshua agrees, nodding. He looks at me, his eyes sparkling. "Throw it!"

I do, and the cylinder goes long, goes impossibly long, drifting in a smooth slide, nearly parallel to the ground below it. Then it hits the edge of the building, and a gust of wind sends it backward and down, circling.

Down, down, down.

It takes what feels like forever for the circle to land in the water.

Joshua and I turn to each other, smiling like little kids. Joshua touches my hair. His fingers rub the end of a rough lock, and then his hand curls gently around the back of my head. His other hand lifts to my waist, and we're kissing.

It's like flying and falling. Like breathing and holding a breath. My heart speeds up, quick drumming in my chest.

His lips are a little chapped. Insistent, pressing against mine. Open in a question I know how to answer.

Then he drops his head with his arms around me, and rests his forehead at the side of my neck, along the top of my collarbone, a familiar gesture. Like we are at the lake and he will next catch me to him, drip cold water onto my shoulders, lift me, and then drop me into the water, both of us laughing, pretending to fight.

Like nothing has changed.

His voice rises, muffled. "Remember the day we climbed on the gym roof and threw airplanes?"

"Of course," I say. I turn my head to press a light kiss into his hair.

"I wish we could just go back." His voice is soft with either shame or longing. I can't tell without seeing his eyes.

"Let's go. I'll buy the tickets. We can take a look at the houses you bought for everyone."

"That's not going back. That's not what . . . " Joshua sighs, a deep defeat.

"Tell me," I urge, pressing my hands into the rigid muscles of his back.

"I'm not good at all this," Joshua says.

It sounds like stage fright, uncharacteristic and new. Words rise to my lips before I can really process a response. The urge to reassure is that strong.

"Says probably the most famous performer in the world," I tease gently. "You can do it. You have before."

"What would you do, Rox?" Joshua asks. "If you could go anywhere. Do anything."

Confusion pulls my eyebrows together, even as I smile at him.

"I'd stay with you. Duh."

Joshua closes his eyes like my answer hurts.

"After that." He shakes his head almost angrily. "You have to want something other than that. That's not enough for you. That's not all of who you are."

I shrug. "I don't know. I don't really think about it."

"Think about it now."

"Get my GED? Go to college, I guess?" I try to imagine it and fail.

An image of Leitzel floats into my mind. Dangling from the top of the circus tent, spinning like an engine propeller.

"I like history," I say.

Joshua takes a breath to say something.

The sliding door hisses open. Artie stands there, glowering.

Joshua and I instinctively break apart like a parent has walked in on us making out.

"Would you like to explain to me," Artie snaps, striding forward, "why the hell you are still awake at nearly dawn the day of what is arguably the most important performance of your career?"

She's wearing yoga pants and a T-shirt, canvas shoes still untied in her rush to get here. Her elbows jut as she props her fists on her hips.

"How—" I start.

"Imagine me, waking early to get a jump on this exceptionally busy and important day," Artie interrupts. "Stepping out onto my balcony and seeing *paper airplanes* float down. Paper. Airplanes."

Joshua rests against the wall, blinking at us like he can't make sense of her sudden appearance or her anger coloring the air.

Then he starts to laugh softly. "Artie. Are you a Birdie?" He stands there, with his arms pulled against his stomach, weakly laughing.

I glance back at Artie. For once she looks completely flummoxed.

Then I notice her shirt. It's official tour merchandise: a black T-shirt with the trademarked logo—outstretched gray-white bone wings, silver-lined, and Joshua's name stenciled across, stitched into and out of and around like tattered feathers.

"Your shirt," I clue her in.

Artie looks momentarily embarrassed. "I lost my Yale shirt last week. Merch table samples were in my room."

Joshua just stands there, laughing slightly.

Artie gestures to me and Joshua, indicating that we should follow her through the living room, where Dan and Rick are asleep. Once inside the bedroom, Artie closes the door. Her cell is in her hand, and she's rapid-fire texting already.

Speed sits up from the bed, rubbing his eyes.

"You can still get three or four hours," Artie says to Joshua. "I'm going to get you a mild sleep aid."

Dr. Meadows. Of course. Three floors down.

"I'm fine," Joshua says.

"You need to sleep."

Joshua slumps against the wall.

"Sorry about that. I must've dozed off." Speed stands and bends over the bed, brushing the coverlet straight.

"It's not a problem." Joshua perches on the edge of the bed. "I like that you got comfortable."

We wait, me and Speed standing, Joshua sitting.

After a moment, Speed flops into the armchair, frowning slightly at Joshua in concern. And I can see it in the drummer's dark eyes, behind the tightly curling lashes, behind the worried assessment of Joshua's wakefulness.

Behind all that, the look that tells me everything I need to know, and why I know I can trust Speed even if I'm not sure about anyone else.

Because Speed has never had a poker face when looking at Joshua. Never.

And Joshua is so spun out, so depleted from every wringing thing, that he needs that pure, unrequited love. Joshua draws from it what he can, which makes the love a vampire sustenance, and it doesn't matter if it's fair to Speed. The intersection of Joshua's need and Speed's friendship and desire are tangled, connected like joint circulation across a shared limb.

From the next room we can hear a blend of voices as Artie answers the suite door.

A polite knock at the bedroom door. I open it, and Dr. Matt comes in, complete with a doctor's bag, like he's in a television show.

"Hey," he says, and he looks fresh, like he expected the call. Maybe he did. It isn't the first.

I don't like him. Dr. Matthew Meadows, but he wants everyone to call him Dr. Matt, like we're all buddies. He joined the tour permanently after Dallas. A small-eyed adult who hasn't admitted how old he is and dresses that way.

Dr. Meadows sits across from Joshua. He murmurs a few vague doctorly *how are you feeling?* questions and takes Joshua's blood pressure.

Then he cuts *I'm being discreet* eyes to Joshua, and clears his throat. "Ahem. Should we step into the bathroom for a private consultation?"

Dr. Meadow's specialty. The primary reason for his retainer. Medicine like magic in the bag, pick out the magic feather that will let you fly.

Or come down to earth, cradled in forced sleep.

Joshua sighs but stands, obediently following Dr. Meadows into the spacious bathroom.

I walk to the bedroom windows and stare down at the pool bar.

Paper airplanes sink into the tranquil water below.

Then it's completely quiet. No murmurs, just silence and running water and more silence.

The bathroom door opens, and Dr. Meadows comes out. He flashes a peace sign and a weak smile. "He should sleep now."

The word *should* hangs in my mind, vague like a picture drawn in sand. *Should*, as in *he has no choice, really. The drug will knock him right out, I'm just saying "should" so that it sounds less drastic.*

We all pretend that it's cool with us.

That the grown-ups are drugging a kid.

"Okeydokey."

Dr. Meadows knows when to leave, I'll give him that.

"I guess I'll be going, too," Speed says.

"Don't be stupid." I smile weakly to cut the sting. "Let's all just crash."

Speed nods and goes to the bed, starts taking extra

pillows off and pulling down the covers. It's a California king—there's plenty of room. He sits on the side and jangles a leg, waiting.

"Shu?" I call, my arms hugging tight across my stomach. After a moment he's there, a hank of raven hair flopped across his eyes.

"It's time to sleep," I say.

Dimmed hazel-green eyes meet mine, a smile that twists like self-recrimination. "Nice work if you can get it."

Speed turns off the light on his side of the bed. He kicks off his shoes. "You just got hired, then."

Joshua laughs a little and shuffles across the room to the bed. He climbs on, moving like an old man with joints made of glass.

Speed lies back, drapes an arm over his eyes. "Night."

I flick out the light in the bathroom and cross to my side of the bed. Joshua lies on his back in the middle, staring up at the ceiling.

I climb in slow, trying not to disrupt the chemical peace.

"What are you doing?" Joshua asks as I lie down. "Both of you. What are you doing here?"

I realize it's not the question of what we're doing in the bed with him.

He wants to know . . . what are you doing here— *with me?*

"Whatever you need, man," Speed says, but his voice

is tired, the words a reflex. His fingers tap lightly against his own collarbones, his need to move, to vibrate, distilled to that one gesture.

"Shhh," I say. "Sleep now. We're here."

A sponge-squeezed laugh wrings out of him. It doesn't have enough force to even shake the bed.

"We're here," he says, quoting me with deep irony. "Where else would we be?"

We lie in a row of three. Separate utensils in the drawer. Silent.

Joshua turns into me, pressing his face close to my neck.

"Tell me about Leitzel again," he whispers.

So I tell him a circus story. About how she would walk out to the center ring, this tiny woman, the star of the Greatest Show on Earth. I whisper about how she would take the rope that hung down from the rigging, tethered high above the audience. How Lillian Leitzel would roll up it, impossibly, but somehow going, wrapping and pulling and lifting, with seeming effortlessness.

Then she would perform there, first on web and trapeze, flipping and twirling, a feather lifted, a fairy ballerina dancing in the air high above the audience.

My hand lifts off his stomach as I rotate my wrist in the air above us, my hand dipping and circling, a gesturing attempt at her grace.

"Everyone loved her," I tell him. "She was the Queen of the Air."

Joshua sighs. His eyelashes brush my neck as he closes his eyes.

"Her life was like an explosion," I continue, repeating his favorite part. "Her friend told her she burned life up, that she would burn it all up. That she should slow down.

"Leitzel replied, 'I'd rather be a racehorse and last a minute than be a plow horse and last forever.'"

Joshua lets out a slow breath. Takes another and lets it out as slowly.

He's asleep.

"She didn't last. But everyone loved her while she did. It was all worth it for her."

8

FAKE GIRLFRIENDS ARE REAL PEOPLE, TOO

A few hours later, Artie arrives with food. It's like a repeat from the night before, except with coffee and hot tea and cereals, eggs, and toast.

While we eat, Artie talks through the day's schedule. Out of deference to the opening night of the tour, there are only a few short stops scheduled. We'll be going to a radio show, where Joshua will have a brief back-and-forth with a shock-jock comedian whose vast audience makes celebrities at least pretend to pay court and "stop by," no matter how much they loathe him.

I watch Joshua as he listens to Artie and doesn't ask any questions.

She talks us through arrival at the arena, costume changes, the show, the after-party. Joshua looks up only once, to nod when she confirms the late-night yacht cruise, the only thing Joshua asked for to celebrate the tour starting.

We've been on a boat like this only a few times before, and each time Joshua swears it's the best sleep he's ever had. Artie was eager to give him something so easy, so tonight, instead of sleeping in the hotel, we'll sleep on a boat anchored off a small island.

It's not really a getaway. But it will have to do.

DeeDee arrives with another assortment of clothes.

Joshua does what they tell him. Changes clothes, waits while they do his hair. He even eats some sugary cereal after Santiago picks it up, handing it to him without a word.

After that, Joshua's personal bodyguard keeps watch at the door. He's scheduled himself to work the whole day and into the night, never taking a shift off, vigilant eyes checking for threats where there are none.

We're all jittery, waiting for the concert.

We're all tired, walking on a thinning tightrope.

Joshua goes to the obligatory press meetings, tapes a radio promo stinger, lets Artie steer him around.

Like he's still sleeping.

In the afternoon, there's a publicity stop that has to look unscheduled. But a few calls have been made, Artie discreetly cueing her favorite vultures to a surprise photo opportunity. Joshua meeting Angel Rey in a restaurant.

She's an actress now, as well as a bubblegum pop star.

A couple of commercials and a TV movie about a wannabe pop star who gets cancer.

Like Joshua, she's a part of the machine, is the machine. Unlike Joshua, she seems to love it. The Good Girl every thirsty teenager and creepy old man wants to turn bad.

Maybe that's why they feel so perfect to the fans as a couple and are a wildly supported OTP, One True Pairing. The shippers call them AngelBird. They think she can help him, that Angel can save him. Can lead the way through the woods of fame, treacherous, dark, and deep.

Her image is just as manufactured as his.

Surprisingly, she's nice enough, Angel Rey, and I can't really hate her. That's not her real name, obviously. They shortened it from Angelique Reyes.

Artie originally set them up while Joshua was rehearsing for the first tour, striking a deal with Angel Rey's manager. Tickets were about to go on sale, and Artie wanted to fuel the fire.

Joshua asked me sit and listen in as Artie explained the date. He looked at me like he was so afraid of how I would take it. Artie made it clear it was "just a PR thing."

"Part of the business," she said.

I didn't say I understood. I didn't let him off the hook, but I didn't dig the hook deeper, either.

He had enough hooks in him already.

I just said, "Do what you gotta do."

A coward's recusal.

The first "date" was at an ice rink. Everyone was there. Her people, his people, the band. The photographers. Even me.

Speed was horsing around on the ice, so I sat on a cold plank of wood next to Ms. Kearney. It was like watching a play. That's what I kept telling myself, as the musicians and dancers fell or gracefully navigated the ice, as Joshua and Angel skated around in slow circles, talking.

She wore a floaty dress, fluttering like butterfly wings.

I wore a gray and black zip-front hoodie over a green flight suit, arms chopped off at the elbows and legs chopped off at the calves.

Angel wore spotless white ice skates, like a professional ice dancer or someone on her way to the Olympics.

My desert combat boots were stained with tar or engine grease.

Joshua and Angel skated in circles and talked. They eventually held hands and struggled to keep from falling and had a sweet-meet-cute-ish first chaste kiss. Like a movie.

Ms. Kearney tried to talk to me about the future, about the book I was supposed to be reading for her, about anything. She reported to Artie about my academic progress weekly, taking her teaching job seriously, even if Artie didn't really care about her own legal guardianship.

Taking me on was just another "part of the business" for Artie.

I met Angel when they came up to the suite, after that first ice-rink date. She was and remains impossibly cute-gorgeous, like an expensive doll—petite, with large dark eyes, perfect skin, dusky dark gold complexion that never breaks out and looks great even under fluorescent lights. I felt sickly looking next to her. Like a surly child in some gothic novel. Gangly and pale with dark smudges under my eyes and hair that looked how I felt: a snarl, always kicking out.

"Rox, this is my friend Angel," Joshua said. Then he gave me a not-for-the-cameras kiss and kept his arms around me after, resting his forehead against my hair, his face turned down to the curve of my neck like an obeisance.

Another of those Ms. Kearney words.

"Nice to meet you," Angel said. "I just wanted to say I understand how it is."

"Me too," I said.

Then she smiled and held out her hand. Her hand was soft in mine, with baby-pink manicured nails and no calluses.

I shook her hand, and so did Joshua.

"I had a nice time, today," she said to Joshua, formally, like a little girl taking leave of an adult, coached in the exactly proper form.

A professional.

"Yeah," Joshua said. "Thanks."

He didn't say, "Me too." He didn't have to, though. His genuine smile, all too rare, spoke for him.

Just part of the business, I told myself.

Since that first date, there have been numerous "sightings" and even a "fight"—which took place when Joshua didn't play the part for once, was barely present. Artie even told the photographers, in a quiet voice and with a practiced roll of her eyes, that they had had their first fight. She didn't say another word, didn't have to. The press ran with it.

He had been partying too much.

He was threatened by her success.

She was smothering him. Gossip blogs got days' worth of clicks out of the pretend drama.

There's a picture of the two of them together. It's the one that gets the most clicks, the most attention, its popularity so overwhelming that you can almost picture legions of eyes scrubbing the digital image until it shines.

It took place right after Joshua's dad died, only a few months ago. Brandon Blackbird had tried contacting Joshua, had even shown up once after a concert, tried getting backstage. He wound up shouting Joshua's name over and over as Santiago forcibly escorted him away.

Joshua wouldn't see him. Wouldn't let him back, wouldn't return his call or read the letters he sent. He'd walked out years before, and he'd never once come back, not until there was money in the picture.

Then Livie'd called a few weeks later to say that his dad was dead. A car, a bottle, predictable pieces of an ugly puzzle.

Joshua paid for the funeral but didn't attend.

Though it started to eat at him from the inside. A grief that was more than half anger, a break that keeps breaking, a microcosmic collapse—little pieces shattering.

That most-circulated picture of AngelBird is from the immediate aftermath of his dad's death.

Artie set it up in a park overlooking a lake. At sunset, the golden hour. Joshua told me about it afterward, because they stood there before the bench where they were supposed to be sitting. Where he was supposed to put his arm around her as they watched the sunset. All so damn symbolic, how can the public *not* see that it's staged?

Watching the Sunset as We Remember Him.

But Angel and Joshua didn't sit. They didn't hug hello—he never intended to hug her. He wanted to tell her this farce of a relationship needed to end.

Instead he stood there before this nice girl, this Angel. You can see Joshua's tension through the long-distance lenses. He's holding himself, arms clamped across his stomach as she stands across from him. Her hands are open as she speaks.

She told him how sorry she was for his loss, for all the losses he carried because of his father.

And that was the trigger. Every hurt rushed to the surface. He'd been hiding from it, from his rejection of his father at the arena and every time after, even hiding his feelings about it from me. He'd had enough of acting, of pretending the weight of his father's death wasn't crippling—the idea that he might have prevented it. This man he barely knew, who he now felt responsible for.

At Angel's words, Joshua curled, his posture collapsing, his arms loosening and tightening across his stomach, his head falling forward as he sobbed. Angel's hands cradling him.

And then the hug.

I've stared at it, too, like everyone else. Birdies reblog and recolor it, superimpose lyrics from their favorite Joshua Blackbird song.

It's always there to be seen anew.

Her eyes closed as her cheek rests against his shoulder.

His arms clinging to her.

When the pictures came out, I told Joshua it was okay before he even saw them. Because for all the dewy Birdie romanticism online, I could see the captured, unscripted moment for what it really was.

Comfort.

Something simple and rare.

We walk into another restaurant, because even Artie is tired, and we eat. The photographers who follow us stop there, too. In fact, most beat us there.

I sit with Speed as the hostess leads Joshua to a table for two. To his seat across from Angel Rey.

They barely talk, although Angel tries. She even touches his hand.

The photographers get their "stolen" shots and leave, and I can predict this latest story spin.

A lover's quarrel, again.

Speed and I are obedient, not moving as the scene wraps up. But Angel sees me and walks over.

We hug, and it's not completely awkward. Just mostly awkward.

Her voice is soft as she stays close and murmurs, "Keep an eye on him, okay?"

She's a real person. I forget that sometimes.

She's not just a cog in the machine, although that's how effortless she makes it all look.

"I'm trying," I answer. Giving the real person the

real truth, no gloss, no Vaseline on the lens or Photoshop aftereffects.

She squeezes my arm and then her entourage arrives, marshaling, escorting, leaving.

Joshua sits slumped at the table, staring out at the impeccable ocean view. Artie shows the photographers out.

I walk over to his table. Speed stays back, although he doesn't have to.

I am a horrible trash heap of a garbage person. I am a Dumpster baby.

Because I cannot help being jealous. Love is limited, always limited, never open, and never undemanding. It's all tangled ropes, a constricting mass of safety harnesses and lines meant only to protect yourself. Love that feels like conditions, like hurting more than helping.

Ropes from him to me, from me to him. Speed, Angel, Artie, the band, Livie and Ty, Dan and Rick, all just tangled ropes.

Nothing is ever safe, even if you think it's controlled.

I could love in a white heat and still consume the thing I claimed to love. I could give myself over to the pyre of that love.

Jealousy gnaws at me, a rat dog snarling at my heels. I can't shake it off.

I sit in the seat where she was, where she touched his hand, and cross my leg, resting my heavy combat boot on my opposite knee. I spread my elbows, taking up all the space I can.

Joshua keeps looking at the ocean, like someone is out there trying to signal him with a mirror. I pick up Angel's barely touched drink. It's something tropical-fruity and tastes like melted candy and cough syrup.

"That went well," Joshua says at last.

I take Angel's leftovers, liquid burning a syrupy trail to my stomach.

9

RADIO KILLED THE
INTERNET STAR

"Thanks for tuning in, LA. We're here with Joshua Blackbird," the radio host—*Chris in the Afternoon!*—purrs into his mic. He's a true LA resident, which means I can't guess his exact age. His face is a little shiny and very taut under his spray tan. Small, intensely white teeth gleam out when he stretches his face to smile.

Our last stop of the afternoon.

I stand with Artie and the bodyguards, watching through glass as Joshua is interviewed, sitting across from Chris in the sound booth.

Artie's arms are rigidly crossed as she watches the clock in the sound booth. It's a five-minute interview only, one Artie would never have scheduled, but the label insisted. Chris has the highest-rated show on Sirius, after all.

"So, you excited about tonight, Joshua?" Chris asks him, stretching his mouth again to smile.

"Absolutely," Joshua says, hitting the line with just enough false enthusiasm that it could be taken for authentic. "I can't wait to get out there. I'm ready."

"So are forty-one thousand fans!"

"I've got the best fans in the world."

Chris laughs. "Your fans are definitely devoted!" He glances at Artie, a small smile and a crooked eyebrow, his expression like running with scissors. "Dude, your fans are *intense*!"

Joshua cuts startled eyes between the host and Artie, standing on the other side of the glass, because it sounds like what it is: a veiled reference.

And I can hear it under the line, the tiny stress fracture. What happened in Dallas, after the show.

I wasn't there. I had gone home for a few days to visit my grandma in Marchant for her birthday.

Joshua was in his hotel room on what was supposed to be a secure floor with a guard posted at the elevator. But it didn't make a difference, and Joshua was alone when it happened.

He's never alone now.

We still don't know how she got the drug. Or how she knew which room was his.

Artie shakes her head at Chris. A warning jerk of her chin.

"They're crazy for you, man. Speaking of which, we have a caller." Chris licks his teeth and pushes a blinking button on the console.

"No!" Artie yells, making me jump, because my brain isn't as quick as hers. I'm always in a fog of exhaustion and chasing-after-it maintenance, so it takes me a minute to process what's happening, even after her shout.

She moves and starts pounding on the locked booth door.

"Joshua?" The caller's voice comes through the speakers.

Chris watches the door, smiling with all his teeth.

Joshua is in shock. At least I think he's in shock. I move to the window and wave at him, then I start to bang on it too. All he has to do is stand up and walk out. All he has to do—

"Yes?" he says, voice faint, stunned.

"I just wanted to say I'm sorry." She sounds younger than she is.

"Hi, Mira." Chris's voice is lush silk. Soothing. A performance of care, of first aid, when he's the one who orchestrated the car crash.

"Hi, Chris," Mira says, still in that small voice.

"Where—" Joshua breathes, the anxiety-squeezed word coming out almost a whisper.

The DJ smooths over it, like a mediator at an

acrimonious divorce. "How's everyone at Haven View, Mira? Taking good care of you?"

"It's fine. I don't like the clothes."

Chris laughs.

Joshua pushes himself back, jerking the headphones off his head. Even through the comforting tinge of Dr. Meadow's Mood Meds, I see it register—

Get OUT.

Joshua's eyes meet mine through the window. I wave urgently, pulling my hand toward myself like I could catch his wrist and pull him through the air. Could pull him up and deliver him safely to the other side of this.

"Joshua?" Mira's words keep him spun out, the shock flattening him to the chair. "I'm so sorry," she says again.

Joshua doesn't reply. A muscle in his jaw jumps as his teeth clench.

"Can you ever forgive me?" Mira asks.

"Get this damn door open *now*!" Artie's voice is rage-sharp.

The radio staff stand to the side, eyes saucer-wide at the drama playing out. Santiago tries the handle of the door.

Chris's voice falls like velvet oil from the speakers. "What do you think, Joshua?"

Joshua is silent. He closes his eyes.

Chris smirks and draws close to his own mic, grand-standing intimacy. "Well, honey," he says to Mira on the line, "it's been what? A year, give or take? Maybe give it some more time."

"Joshua." Mira's voice, insistent. "I need you to forgive me. Please."

"What'd you do, exactly?" Chris asks. "Beyond slipping him a roofie, taking some selfies, and stabbing him when he tried to get help?" He laughs. Then, suddenly serious, "Are there more pictures, Mira? Ones we didn't see?"

Joshua's eyes snap open. "Mira," he says, leaning forward.

"Yes?"

Santiago braces his shoulder against the door—then he batters it—an immense slam audible over the speakers.

"Listeners, someone is trying to interrupt our conversation," Chris says.

"Shut up, Chris," Mira says. "No one wants to hear you." Her voice has lost some of its childlike lilt—an edge buried underneath like a razor under the skin of an apple.

Santiago smashes into the door again. It groans but doesn't give.

"Yes, Joshua?" Mira prompts.

Joshua looks at me. His eyes dark with understanding. Even if he walks out right now, it's not going away. The Miras of the world will keep surfacing. Chris and those like him will dredge swamps for the bloated corpse.

Santiago leans back and kicks the door. It flies open with a bang.

Artie rushes into the room. She grabs the mic from the DJ, pushing him back.

"Mira!" she snaps. "This is Artemis Malfa. You're breaking the conditions of your plea bargain. Put an attendant on the phone. Now!"

"No."

Chris just sits back, wearing a grin that flies would swarm over.

Artie scans the deck of buttons and lights on the table before her.

"Listeners," she says, "this program is in violation of a court-mandated restraining order and should be considered not only illegal but potentially damaging to the parties involved. It's also in the poorest taste. I urge you to listen to another station."

She punches a series of buttons until the speaker cuts out and the ON THE AIR sign dims.

"Hey! We're live!" Chris says.

"Not anymore." Artie stabs a finger at him. "You're a piece of—"

"You knew the game when you walked in the studio today."

"You'll rot," Artie hisses.

Chris laughs. "Easy, honey."

Artie touches Joshua's shoulder. "Let's go."

Joshua stands, looking sick.

"Have a great show tonight, kid." Chris says. "Really. Break a leg. Everyone's cheering for you!" The DJ leans back in his tilting chair and starts clapping, loud and mocking.

"You'll hear from our lawyers, and the police," Artie says.

Chris puts his headphones back on as Artie steers Joshua out of the booth. "I'll just pay a fine, if that. Public interest, fair game."

Artie doesn't reply, putting an arm around Joshua's back and guiding him away. Santiago takes point, forehead lowered, coldly furious.

I fall in behind Artie as the other guards take up positions around us.

We're a tiny phalanx, a battered strike team retreating, and I can't stop the image from taking hold in my mind, this image of us with shields, spears, and helms, as we barrel down the radio station hall, through the door into reception, past the secretary and others waiting, past the cell phone cameras and devouring eyes.

Everyone heard it.

The speakers throughout the building snap on, and the radio's stinger plays as we move down the hall. Then Chris's voice falls, soothingly, welcoming listeners back, apologizing for the interruption.

Joshua keeps his head ducked. Artie, our commander, keeps propelling him.

Walking wounded, help the stretcher cases.

Santiago mashes the elevator button, and his eyes dart around, looking for a target to hit. The elevator dings as Chris starts replaying the interview.

Then we're in, down, out to the stretch SUV. We pile in, and Santiago orders the driver to burn rubber, and we're pulling into traffic as if something is chasing us.

The car speeds, and I'm gasping at a fast corner. Until I look at Santiago.

He's so angry his eyes are snapping. He holds utterly still, keeps checking Joshua.

The speed isn't from Santiago's anger, or from fear of a threat. Of course not.

The speed is for Joshua. To put actual physical distance between him and the voice on the radio.

I glance at Joshua.

He's huddled against the window—looking out. It's only because I'm sitting right next to him that I can feel the slight shiver, just one, that creeps through his rigid stillness.

Artie is barking into the phone, call after call, deploying lawyers. Seeking suppression of the recording of the program, at least officially. Ordering the filing of papers in court about the break of the Do Not Contact provision.

Appointing a point person to involve the local police, coordinate them with the court in Dallas.

She's a machine, a tank, guns blazing. Demonstrating firepower.

Joshua has gone utterly still. His hand closest to me rests on his leg.

I reach out and take it. It's cold and slack. He doesn't move.

10

ONSTAGE

When we arrive at the hotel, we get out and take up the phalanx again. Artie is still on the phone. Added bodyguards meet us at the car, cushioning us from the people, the lobby-hanging paparazzi ready for us.

Joshua doesn't even put on his sunglasses. Doesn't pull up the hoodie, or hunch like he normally does when running the lobby gauntlet.

Questions are thrown at him as cameras click and flash.

Joshua marches, he *marches*, without looking to either side, directly to the elevator. The doors open, and Speed is standing in it wearing unlaced shoes like he stuffed his feet into them in a rush.

"I heard it," Speed says to me, quietly, once we're all

in the elevator. "Everyone did. I knew the lobby would be packed." He bounces slightly on his toes while we ride up.

Joshua doesn't acknowledge anyone. Just stares at the closed doors until they open on our floor, and we walk to the suite.

Once the door closes behind us, Artie starts to talk to him, spewing all her anger at the DJ, how she is going to bury him, how she's going to protect Joshua, how "that sicko" in the institution is never getting out, and what's more, her doctors—

Joshua turns his back on her and sits in the deep armchair that faces the windows, the kingdom of Los Angeles lying below.

Artie falters in her rapid-fire word triage, glancing at me and then Speed for explanation.

Joshua pulls earphones out of his pocket, plugs them into his phone, and then places the buds into his ears.

He looks at his phone for a moment, selecting music. Then he looks out the window again, letting his hands and head slouch to rest in the cushion-swallowing chair.

Artie snaps her mouth shut and then goes into the bedroom, summoning Joshua's phone-in therapist back in Georgia through the voice recognition on her phone.

As if he will be able to do anything just by talking to Artie.

Speed and I glance at each other. He swipes a hand down his face, like he's easing off a cobweb of tension.

He pulls a chair over to sit nearby, facing the windows.

"You can go," Joshua says, voice slightly louder than necessary, speaking over the noise in his head.

He doesn't look at me.

"Rox too. Just go." Then he glances at Santiago, to make sure the bodyguard is still there.

As close as he gets to alone.

"Okay," I say, and I don't know where to go.

"Come on, Rox," Speed says. And his calling me Joshua's nickname pulls needles into my eyes.

I follow Speed out.

We head to Speed's room and collapse across the beds. And time passes. We watch cartoons, avoiding the news shows, and talk, stilted utterances of shock and concern and *what will happen?* I even wonder if the tour might be cancelled or postponed, a lone flare of hope—

"No, it won't," Speed says. "This doesn't change anything."

And of course he's right. Nothing has changed, and Artie will think that *work* is what Joshua needs.

He needs the opposite. A break. To go somewhere he can be himself and let go. He needs time away from this circus where he is the star attraction.

The sun sets outside, a glory of umber. We should be

leaving to go to the arena, but we sit until the last hint of pink leaves the night sky.

Time crawls by. Speed and I talk less, exchanging worried looks. Glancing at our watches. What is Joshua doing? Is Artie talking to him? Should we go back up to his suite?

The concert has to have started, the opening band going on even though the headliner hasn't arrived yet.

Even though we're watching TV in a hotel room, I imagine I can hear the crowd cheering for the opening band, or waiting at the end of their set. As instruments get changed out, as interim music blares over the speakers.

Are we even going?

Then Speed's phone goes off and we're summoned.

Down in the lobby, we wait for Joshua. The stretch SUV is in the circle, waiting to drive us to the arena.

The elevator opens, and the phalanx comes, Joshua wearing the same clothes, earbuds in, mask of impassivity still on.

It stays on in the car, through the arrival at the arena, a throng of pushing fans screaming his name, screaming love. We wind through them, through doors, sets of doors, doors after doors after doors.

And then Joshua is stripping off his slouchy street clothes and putting on one of the crisp sets of stage clothes, new and inky dark, silver accents so he shows up onstage.

Then DeeDee is hovering before him, styling his hair and putting on stage makeup—dark-smudged eyes, shadowing cheeks and eyelids, a dab of color on his lips.

And he's dressed, and ready, more quickly than anyone.

Speed's ready, just going to go on in his shorts and muscle-T. The drum kit shields him from the audience, anyway. I grab an eyeliner pencil from DeeDee's holster and hold it up in front of his face.

The lead guitarist, Quinn, is still wrestling with his mesh shirt.

Joshua stands with his eyes closed, waiting, listening to the music in his head.

Speed waits, and I draw a crisp line all the way around his dark eyes, just so that it feels like he's getting something, not just demands. Not just dregs.

He offers a small smile in response.

Quinn is ready, and the others as well. Joshua doesn't even glance back at me, so I stay. Why would I go? There's nowhere to wait up there, and we have to go through everyone—

He's gone. They're fighting their way to the stage.

I fall on one of the sofas and watch the giant TV that will project the show into the greenroom.

Tonight should even be more polished than usual. A film crew is here to get live footage of Joshua's new song—a performance video to release first.

Feed the machine.

The stage is dark, the roar is percussive.

The show begins.

"Screw this day," Artie snaps, ripping her phone out of her ear.

As if that's a cue, the few people still milling around quickly exit.

I stay on the sofa.

Artie prowls to the craft services table and pours herself a large Scotch.

The show goes on.

And of course, Joshua hits every mark. So much so that I'm not sure if he's acting. So much so that I wonder if performing is bringing him out of it, out of the fugue or isolation or whatever it is that he's fallen into.

From backstage, watching on the big screen, opening night feels like a TV show . . . not something that's really happening just a few sets of doors and halls away. The songs cascade out of the speakers like a perfect playlist of his hits, the newer songs cocooned in between proven favorites.

At the halfway mark, Joshua disappears from the stage for a costume change. The drum kit rolls forward as Speed takes a blistering solo, and then begins a call and response with the audience.

The crowd shrieks loud enough that it sounds like a

distant thunder in the greenroom. On the screen, I watch as a large set piece, huge scaffolding like a cage wall, lowers onto the stage. Dancers rush to it and stop, freezing in the act of reaching to climb.

The stage goes dark. A single spotlight sweeps the crowd, then tilts up.

Joshua hovers on nearly invisible wires high above the cage wall. He's changed from the black clothes into blinding white. As he sings, the rig lifts and lowers him, swooping movements like flight. The dancers below climb toward him, reaching to grab and pull him down.

The song ends when one succeeds in grabbing his feet, and they spin, lowering to the stage. The dancers form a wall around him, shielding as they remove the harness.

The second half of the show goes perfectly, Joshua showing no sign of fatigue or stress, actually seeming to enjoy himself, giving himself over to the performance.

He sings the last song of the set, and the show's over.

The band leaves the stage for a few minutes of wardrobe changes and swigs of sports drinks. The crowd, knowing the game, applauds nonstop, encouraging an encore that was never in doubt.

And then the band reemerges to a rising swell of victorious screams.

Two high-production encore songs later, Joshua and

the band bow, wave, and return the audience's applause. They turn their backs and descend backstage for good.

But Joshua doesn't follow them. He leans in to say something to Speed, then stands there, not moving. The spotlight continues to reflect off his back. The audience begins a rhythmic chant, small and disorganized at first, then taking shape; "Blackbird," screamed in an accelerating beat. The words fly around the arena, and crescendo into a unified scream as Joshua stands motionless.

Someone hands Joshua his acoustic guitar. And then Joshua turns, alone, small on the otherwise empty stage.

Another roadie emerges, walking a stool over to the mic. The crowd erupts. Joshua takes a seat and tunes the guitar, and all the noise suddenly disappears as if swallowed.

Artie and I are just as silent, mesmerized as we watch. Joshua's never done this before.

His fingers strum the guitar strings, a progression of chords and notes I recognize, but I can't remember where or why. The sound is gentle at first, soothing. Then an intensity builds and the sound begins taking shape—a simple chord progression with minors and flats, accentuated with a slide up the neck of the guitar. A blues riff, raw and powerful.

Just before Joshua sings the first note, the pieces tumble into place and I recognize the song. The very first version of "Armored Heart" he played for me; the first version of his first song. He plays and sings like he's alone, the music spare, intimate. Forty thousand people are breathless.

As the last note dissolves, Joshua hangs his head, almost in supplication. The crowd erupts as one, standing, thunderous.

I have never seen Joshua look so small.

11

THE FUN MARATHON

Everyone gets cleaned up in their dressing rooms, and we pile into massive stretch SUVs to go to the after-party.

The band and the dancers talk about the VIPs they saw in the audience, and which famous actor or actress they hope to see at the club. They talk about what they packed to take onto the yacht afterward, for their day off, the one-day cruise Artie has arranged, which will be an overnight trip to some island.

Then the yacht will turn around and come back, and the tour will hit the road the very next day.

It's supposed to be a celebration. Yet Joshua appears drained.

The party at the club is itself an unstoppable force. And the star's mood doesn't matter, because this party is as much for the crew, the corporate sponsors, and the select VIPs.

Speed tries to get next to Joshua, saying that we can go back to the hotel if we want, and skip everything. Even the yacht.

Joshua nods but doesn't move, acknowledging the option but choosing not to pursue it.

Then Artie arrives and takes him by the elbow, and we're on the move again. The party is private and packed, the space rented out and filled by select guests. Hollywood figures, their entourages, tour roadies, the musicians, the dancers, and us.

Speed and I shadow Joshua and Artie, a circuit of tables and handshakes, Joshua just letting Artie guide him through the motions. Another performance.

Finally we're in the booth, elevated, behind a velvet rope, and Santiago is there, a somewhat paternal wall of muscle.

Except not a parent, because he looks the other way when needed.

Joshua just sits, isolated in the distance he's pulled around himself in spite of the crowd. I sit next to him but he still feels like he's not really there. The gap between us is only inches, but inches count when you're trying to catch someone flying through the air.

Or falling.

Speed sits next to me. We sip our drinks and wait for Joshua to find his way back to us.

Speed holds my hand. The music changes, and now it's one of Angel Rey's club songs, light and frothy, bubbling like a fizzing drink.

"Let's dance!" Speed yells in my ear. He tugs at me like a little kid wanting to ride the merry-go-round.

The bass thumps suddenly in my joints, and I feel the need too. Just to move my body, and be a part of something.

Not apart from everything.

The energy is a frustration, a longing for release. I need to move.

"Yes!" I yell in reply to Speed, and turn to Joshua, to try to help him move, too. "Dance with us."

"I prefer it here," Joshua says.

"No, we have to *dance*," I yell.

Joshua shrugs, and I kiss his cheek to tell him it will help. Just keep moving.

Speed can't hold still anymore. He pushes the people on the other side of him—who are these people?—in the booth, and they're laughing and getting out ahead of us. I'm attached to Speed ahead of me, and Joshua behind me, through my linked hands. We're children on a field trip.

Hold on to your buddy, children. Don't get lost. Hold on.

Santiago falls in behind Joshua, the chaperone caboose.

The dancers on the floor are jumping like beads of water on a subwoofer, bouncing to the beat, screaming and celebrating or exorcising, in unison.

They make a path for us.

The lights scatter, whirl, as machine-made fog drifts down over the dance floor.

There's universal acclaim that we're here. And it's not just for Joshua being on the dance floor. It's for me too.

Because I'm here. I brought him. I've captured his wrists and pulled him through.

I suddenly think of Lillian Leitzel. This party is like the ones she went to, the dancing and drinking and excess, all the beautiful people there for love of her.

Here for love of Joshua Blackbird.

"Hey, gorgeous!" a dancer shouts at me. Cristal. Her name is Cristal, I remember, like the champagne. She's undulating in front of me, looking at me, and she's so beautiful. Like there are points of warm light from her to me, from her chest, from her eyes, her hips.

I smile at her because I like the way she looks at me.

Speed and I laugh and dance with her, and I turn to pull Joshua closer and realize that he's marking time, dancing at the edge of the dance floor.

Joshua is moving slow. He could dance any way he wants, could match every ace move being pulled or attempted on the floor.

But he's contained. Like he's balancing a cup on his head, and if he moves too fast, something will spill on him.

Or spill out from him.

He's not looking at anyone. His head is up, and his gaze is fixed over our heads, in the middle distance.

I move to him and notice the not-accidental brushes, bumps, and jostles he absorbs. How everyone on the floor near him deliberately dances into him, brushing against him, hands that reach out, just briefly, or more lingering. How he is this thing—

Thing.

—everyone wants a piece of. A touch of. Like a talisman.

Santiago stands behind him and to the side. An unmoving rock in the dance floor current.

It was wrong, pulling Joshua onto the floor. I tell myself he could have said no, could have stayed in the booth, but I don't believe myself.

"Hey, Shu." I touch his arm, and he stops his slow moving and looks down at me.

His eyes tired, empty.

"Let's leave," I yell.

Something moves behind his eyes. I can't recognize it. He doesn't say anything, just nods quickly.

I push my fingers through his and grip tight.

"I've got you, Joshua," I tell him. "I got you."

His forehead falls to my shoulder, like we are at the lake

back in Marchant, being jostled by the wake of speedboats and Jet Skis, instead of a crowd.

Then Artie is there, and she's grabbing me, and Speed, and she's telling our inner crew that it's time to go to the next party.

"We're done," I yell for the both of us. She nods.

"Don't worry," Artie yells at Joshua, "I'm taking you to where you can rest."

We throng out, pile into the stretch SUV. Joshua sits by the door, gazing out the window, and Artie has managed to snag the seat next to him. Others are also there, crowding into the space and air.

I sit next to Santiago.

The car winds away from the city, into the posh mansions that surround it, that crowd the water, regal against commanding ocean views.

Then we're pulling through a heavy swinging gate and stopping at one of the mansions.

Artie leads the way, pulling Joshua out of the limo and saying, "Ta-da!" like a magician.

Joshua extricates himself from Artie's grip and takes in the mansion before us.

"Where are we?" he says.

Artie sweeps a hand at the mansion. "This is the mansion you bought for yourself! Remember? I offered to furnish it for you. Welcome home!"

She's smiling like this is the biggest thing ever.

As far as I can see, it's just another hotel. Nothing about this enormous place says "home."

Joshua gives her a weak smile. "Thanks, Artie. I'm sure it's great."

Her eyes widen in surprise at the mild thanks for all her effort. But she plays it off anyway. "Only the best," she says. "Wait till you see it."

She takes us on a tour of the place, room after room. So many bedrooms and bathrooms I lose count, all furnished luxuriously, expensive-looking knickknacks and art, marble floors, hallways, sweeping staircases, a library, a movie theater, a terraced backyard with an expansive pool—a breathtaking view of the dark ocean, the moon glowing like a gentle spotlight you could touch.

The yard slants down, and there's a dock and a yacht anchored there, lighted and with the buzzing activity of a white-shirted crew.

"And *that's* for tonight," Artie says, with a particular note of pride in her voice. "Just like you asked. The ocean to rock you to sleep, Joshua. Tomorrow's a full day off."

"Thanks, Artie," Joshua says. "Thanks for arranging everything."

We walk down the steps, down the winding walk to the dock, to the yacht. Just a small group of us this time.

Joshua and me and Speed, Artie and Santiago, and a few other security guys.

Santiago climbs onto the stern of the boat with ease and disappears to perform a security check.

We walk up the ramp set at the midline of the boat. A crew member introduces herself as Mattie and offers a quick tour and safety briefing. She stares at Joshua and then, catching herself doing it, forces herself to look away.

Joshua accepts, so we trail Mattie to the top level, where the lavish bedrooms are, then down to the sitting rooms, the bar, the media room.

Mattie takes us to the sundecks fore and aft, the latter lower to the water. She shows us the ladder they'll put overboard tomorrow so we can swim in the ocean after we've dropped anchor at the private lagoon.

She shows us the life rings and life preservers, tells us about emergency procedures, then displays the scuba equipment stowed in the benches at the back of the boat. She shows us the portable bar cart and the sunshade they will unfurl tomorrow, when we rest in our skins under the sun.

The crew stand at attention as we pass or murmur soft greetings as they prepare to disembark.

"We're going to cruise out slow tonight, roughly forty nautical miles," the captain says as we pass the wheelhouse again. "We'll weigh anchor near a dive buoy sometime in the predawn, so the engines will fall silent. Don't be alarmed.

In the morning you can dive a bit, if you like, then we'll continue to the lagoon for your lunch."

Artie thanks him, and we all move to our separate rooms at the top of the boat. A crew member yells, "All ashore who are going ashore."

But we're all staying.

The engines thrum to life, and the ropes are loosed, a crew member nimble as a monkey jumping from the dock to the boat deck as it begins to move away.

"Do you remember which one is ours?" Joshua asks me, pinching his eyes as he leans against the doorway.

I take his hand and lead him back. We pass the room Speed will use next to Santiago's, right next to ours.

Santiago follows us.

"I'll be right here, Mr. Blackbird," he says, indicating his door catty-corner to ours.

"It's okay. Get some rest, Santi."

We go into the bedroom and collapse across the bed. I ruck up the edge of the bedspread and pull it over us like a taco shell; we're both too tired to get under it properly.

The thrum of the engines is a hum of movement, nothing more, a murmuring telling us to sleep. To rest.

"We made it," I say.

"Hooray for us," Joshua whispers.

I curl around his arm, tucking my chin above his shoulder.

I squeeze him, pulling my arm tight over his stomach. Glance up at his face, which looks so sad it takes me by surprise.

"I'm sorry," I offer.

He kisses my cheek. "You have nothing to be sorry for."

He shakes his head and then he hugs me, squeezing long arms across and around my back and side, turning toward me as he lowers his forehead to my shoulder, and the engines churn the water that will take us far away.

I hold him there, stroking the short hair on the crown of his head. His breath is uneven over my collarbone, his arms wrapped tight across the small of my back.

"I'm the sorry one, Rox." His voice is tight. "About this tour. About *all* this crap—"

"Shhh," I murmur, like he's a wounded creature. My hands on his hair and back are light, stroking reassurance. "It's okay. Go to sleep. I'll be here. Sleep."

And I'm thinking, *Without a pill. Real rest, for once. Let the ocean work its magic.*

And then, like a miracle, it does. His breathing grows regular, the arms clinging to me loosen, and he tips slightly back, sleeping.

At last. I let my arm rest, and sleep comes for me as well.

Later, I hear the engines turn off, and the silence is like a sacred hush after all the noise of the day. I barely wake for it, just notice it in passing, like I notice Joshua's quiet weight and heat beside me.

The waves rock me right back to sleep.

In my dream, I hover above the night-dark ocean. I'm flying, spinning through the air like Lillian Leitzel. I sense Joshua with me, moving in the air somewhere, but I can't see him. So I spin and flutter, weightless.

Then something unseen snaps. A sudden break like a gunshot, jarring my arm, and suddenly the air can't hold me anymore.

I plummet, the wind snatching the screams from my mouth. I flail into empty air, reaching for something, for hands, for a harness, for a net.

Nothing will save me.

As I hit the water, I jerk awake, heart drumming with a jolt of inhalation. I feel cold and sweaty at the same time.

I reach out for Joshua, for the feel of something solid, real.

The air around me is empty. The mattress beside me is cool to the touch.

Joshua is gone.

12

ORPHEUS'S LAST LYRIC

The yacht is still as predawn light tinges the sky. I tamp down the panic, a nightmare residue. Dampen the fear that Joshua isn't beside me.

He's fine. He's watching TV or something.

I can't remember exactly where the media room is, so I start searching as if the yacht were a maze, just keep making right-hand turns every chance I get. At first I knock on doors lightly before I open them, but after a while and nothing but sleeping heads, I stop knocking and just crack open each door silently.

Speed is asleep. Santiago isn't in his room, although his bed is mussed. His bag sits unzipped on the floor, deflated like he's unpacked it into the drawers nearby.

I keep my search up, from deck to deck, moving faster and faster.

He's with Santiago. They're together, talking or just watching the water.

"Joshua!" I yell, because my heart won't listen to reason.

My heart knows something is wrong.

I dash down the steps and outside onto the aft deck, where we are supposed to lie on the cushions or dive with canned air strapped to our backs. Where we are supposed to rest and find peace.

Relief. A single towel sits on one of the bench cabinets. Joshua's shirt next to it. He went swimming.

The ladder is in the water. It knocks gently against the side of the aft deck with the swells. The water is empty as far as the eye can see.

I lift Joshua's T-shirt. His cell phone rests on the bench under it. My fingers grow numb.

"Shu?" I call. My voice sounds sharp and fear-raw. The only reply remains the hollow slap-slap of waves against the boat.

Why would he go into the water alone? He wouldn't, I realize. Santiago follows him like a shadow.

Still, I rush to the top deck, squinting out into the dawn-dark water. I call his name until my voice is raw, searching in the empty water around the boat. My fear is a wave, still building up power and speed.

I shout for Santiago now. Over and over. Still nothing.

Joshua was always a careful swimmer, back home, at the lake. Neither of us ever had lessons.

We always stayed close to land. We always stayed together.

He would dunk me, splashing when I came up. Or we'd hold hands, floating on our backs like river otters, water sloshing cool across our stomachs.

He'd catch me, he'd shake his head, and his hair would shed droplets like a rain shower. He'd put his forehead low on my shoulder. We'd feel the wake of the speedboats out in the deep of the lake, the waves rocking us as they raced to shore.

I stare at the peaceful waves, waiting for something to break the surface of the water, for a raven-haired head to emerge, shaking off the dripping water, a smile lighting up that face, laughing at my nightmare fears.

Silence.

And now I'm moving through sludge, holding his phone. But I'm moving toward the water.

Arms grab me and a sun-darkened face, clean, with a wide, smooth forehead, presses into my view. Mattie, the crew member who gave us the tour, holds me back.

"What's wrong?" she asks. "Why the shouting?"

"Josh-sh-shua," my voice stutters. I've started to shake with dread. "He went into the water. May-maybe Santiago was with him."

Mattie hears me say it, looks past me at the ladder, bobbing slightly with the aft deck in the water. Sees the towel and his shirt on the bench. She snaps a radio off her belt and calls the captain.

"Man overboard."

It's surreal, like a movie sound effect, but a Klaxon blares and crew members assemble. Mattie orders two of them into the transport dinghy. The motor starts with a submerged roar, and they take off to search in the water, going first around the boat and then back the way that we came.

Suddenly the deck is crowded with activity, with people, most in white shirts, but soon the band is here, with panic stamped on their faces.

Speed stands beside me. His arms are crossed tightly as he holds completely and uncharacteristically still. As if willing with all his being, every molecule, for Joshua to appear. Motionless with the contained energy of silent, desperate prayer.

Activity churns around us.

Santiago finally arrives, frowning like an angry god holding thunderbolts. I feel worse at the sight of him. Because he is alone. Because he shouldn't be. I run to him, crying, raging. "You're supposed to protect him!" I pound his tree-trunk chest with balled-up fists. "He's gone! Where were you?" He pulls me toward him and wraps me in an embrace.

"Whoa, whoa, there. He's probably fine. Just gone out for a swim." But his voice sounds hollow.

"When was the last time you saw him?"

Santiago is silent for a second that feels like an eternity. Then he sighs. "Last night, Roxanne. With you. I went to sleep right away and was out of it."

Artie arrives, firing rapid questions, the long sheet of her bleach-blond hair tucked into the neck of the shirt she hurriedly pulled on.

The same excruciating conversation begins again, this time with Artie, painful seconds slipping through, each one stealing breath from my lungs. Every moment that he doesn't arrive, laughing from having fooled us, or surprised at our concern, is a lead weight dragging on my frantic heart.

"Maybe someone took him back to the house," Artie is saying. "We're not that far out." She turns and gazes at the empty water, as if she could see the mansion she decorated for him across from us, waiting to do her bidding.

Waiting to open its doors and spill him out.

The crew members confirm what I already know: no one took him back to the house. No one left the boat. No one saw him. They dropped anchor near the buoy, and after that only the night crew was on, a watchman and the first mate. No one saw Joshua at all.

I stare daggers at Santiago even though he looks

stricken. Also, it's not like he is paid to watch Joshua sleep. If that was anyone's job, it was mine.

My breath saws, ragged at the thought. Frantic pain wrenches my heart.

I'd give anything to lose this sinking feeling in my gut. The others look frantic, but no one's losing it like I am.

The captain organizes a search of the yacht, above and below decks, crew areas and engine room, while we wait for the dinghy to return.

The search of the boat is efficient and thorough. Joshua is not there.

The dinghy returns; there is no sign of Joshua. No sign of anyone. No sign of anything other than swells and chop.

"Is that a real camera?" Artie asks, voice sharp as she points to a tinted opaque bubble above the deck.

Then we're all walking, following Artie, who's following the captain to the bridge and the electronics wall behind it. There are only a few cameras on the yacht, mostly on the decks and in the engine room and kitchen. Motion activated and for security and liability purposes only, he assures us, as he pulls the footage up on the computer.

We watch time race backward. All of us rewinding though the nightmare of our activity in the dawn, now day.

He rewinds back to near dark and stillness.

I see myself on the screen, sobbing, moving with rapid abruptness backward from the deck as I am rewound, rewound, until I disappear and the deck is empty.

The towel and the shirt rest over the phone, a still picture waiting for the hands that will pick them up, put them back the way they were.

A blip as the motion sensor is activated, and he's there. A head in the water, receding. Then rewinding closer. Then swimming, then floating. Rewound onto the ladder, rewound onto the deck.

What was he thinking?

My ears are ringing, and I don't remember gripping the chair back in front of me, but I am, curling into myself, into this injury. A sob clawing its way up to my mouth, ripping hook-sawed breaths from my lungs.

My voice whispers his name. My voice comes before my tears, in slow motion, in a moment of time reversal, time stoppage, time restart-rewind—why is this moment so long? This moment a held breath, burning in my chest like an arrested scream.

Then the tears are there, and I can't see past them, can't register anything other than the shocked noises of the others around me, sounds of grief and disbelief as we try to watch, as the yacht's captain rewinds to before—

Then he hits Play.

And the horrible moment enacts itself again. A tragic time capsule of a moment before it was too late.

For just an instant, the screen is blank. Then a blip, and a time stamp appears on the lower corner, 4:15 A.M. Then a head, Joshua's passing close beneath the camera and triggering its motion sensor. We watch on the screen as he climbs down the steps to the aft deck.

He stands, staring out into the water for what feels like a long time.

Then he disappears for a moment and returns with a towel. He shakes the towel open and drops it on the bench.

On the screen in front of us, Joshua bends and carefully places his cell phone on the bench. Then he stands and pulls his shirt over his head.

Beside me, I hear Speed murmur a denial, like he could speak to this image of someone we love, could make him stop. Could make him understand the danger.

Could make him turn back.

Then Joshua looks away from the ocean, looks back at the boat. Maybe he heard something.

After holding still for a moment, he smiles.

It's a strange, indecipherable smile. It changes as you watch. First it's the open smile of a kid sneaking out at night. The smile of climbing into my bedroom window while trying to be quiet, and failing utterly.

The smile from Marchant. Eager.

That smile I haven't seen in so long; it lights up my heart in pain and love, sending spears into my belly and my chest. Into every limb.

But then it changes, and the smile becomes sad. A smile like falling. Like a weight, like sorrowful knowledge.

Joshua turns his back on me, on the camera, and faces the open ocean.

Then he walks to the deck edge. He pulls the ladder out and places it in the water, taking a moment to make sure it is connected to the boat deck correctly, so he'll have a way back.

Back onto the boat. Does he plan to return?

Then he turns and climbs down it halfway. He sits on the deck. His shoulders heave with deep breaths twice as his head falls forward a moment.

Is the water cold?

His arms tuck in, like mine do now as I watch him, a cradling of self.

Then quickly, without looking back, he pushes away from the deck into the Pacific water.

I can imagine him whooping, or gasping. Or laughing, or crying—all are possible after that smile.

He paddles in the water, visible for a moment. He floats on his back, and I can't see his feet. I think he has them tucked into a rung of the ladder so he won't float away.

Then he sits up in the water, head and shoulders just visible. He swims back and forth, doing a lap parallel to the aft deck.

Then he turns and swims out, away from the deck lights, into the night-black water.

Away from the boat. Away from even the dive buoy, a blinking light to the left of the boat. Striking out with assured strokes, Joshua swims away as if he knows where he's going. What he's doing.

The back of Joshua's head is just visible for one final moment. And then it can't be seen at all.

He disappears behind the drawn curtain of the night.

The pain is startling; it's physical, deep in my body like I can feel my heart snapping, a wet, rupturing break. Then every sob claws its way out of the pieces, talons of self-annihilating grief, and I'm lost to it.

A crew member next to me curses and murmurs a prayer.

Then they're searching again, back in the small boat. Other crew members are donning scuba gear.

Speed's voice breaks through my haze.

"He would have left a note." His tone says what his words stop short of saying. What none of us has voiced aloud. *If he had planned on killing himself.*

Artie steps close to him. Her manicured hands alight

on either side of his face, pulling him down to look down at her. Making him listen.

"We'll find him."

The fear in her eyes says we won't.

Speed yanks his head away. He takes two steps back and then turns, racing away from us. From this moment.

There is an ongoing jabber of incomprehensible voices, giving orders or sobbing, looking at tide and current charts, trying to determine a direction for our desperate search.

I hear their voices, Artie's and Santiago's. The words fall into my ears like a malediction.

Why, we should have, we didn't, why—

It's a litany now, a last-list prayer, confession: What should I have done? What should any of us have done? To protect him, even from himself?

The curse of the knowledge, this time-stuck moment of hell. This is hell. This moment is hell—and it's real, and it's here on earth, and if hell has layers, this is the center of it.

Speed walks back into the crowded room, dragging his feet like he can barely keep himself upright. He weeps, his face a mask of anguish.

Joshua's notebook is in his hand.

He holds it out to me.

I take it. Remember Joshua scrawling in it, time after time. Racing hand to keep up with racing thoughts.

I open it, flipping backward from the end, blank pages fluttering by. Until I see Joshua's handwriting scrawling out in uneven lines:

Orpheus's Last Lyric

No path, can't see the way
End of days, everyone pays
I'd say good-bye, I'd say good-bye
A moving target the final verse
No longer fighting—this isn't a curse
Don't be angry, this isn't sad—
All it takes is all I had.
No path, can't see the way
Just more reasons
Everyone pays
Can't get away, can't get free
Can't see another possibility
Go home, go home
Sweet one, go home.
I'd say good-bye, I'd say good-bye
Forget that you knew me
Or remember you did—
If you were looking, I never hid.
Forget that you knew me
Or run far away

Perhaps we'll meet again—
Someday.
I am—
Not singing but howling—
Not waving but drowning—
Not flying but falling—
Not going home—
Just going away.
I'd say good-bye
I'd say good-bye
Good-bye before I change you
Good-bye before I hurt you
Good-bye before we met
Good-bye always good-bye—
Easier than Forget

"No, no, no." My voice sounds like a breath, chanting a prayer against what I know. What I feared.

13

CAPSIZED

Hours pass. The Pacific sun bright and warm, the ocean sparkling, winking. A perfect day, and I can't wake from this nightmare.

The divers and the crew in the dinghy return, with no sign of Joshua.

The Coast Guard joined the search effort a while ago. The ship's captain is talking about currents and statistics, how easy it is to become disoriented in the water. How easy to misjudge and become tired. To get a cramp, to panic, and to submerge.

Artie nods, absorbing the words. She looks at me.

"We have to let them know," she says.

Ty and Livie.

A sob that sounds like a cough chokes out of Speed. I'm clinging to him, our hands squeezing pinch-tight in an urge to come awake. Come awake.

Speed fights the words out. A forlorn hope. "But. Isn't it too soon? There's still a chance . . ."

At that, Artie breaks down. Something I've never seen, never before this moment. Even when she had pneumonia during tour and didn't miss a day, and dealing with the aftermath of Dallas. She didn't stop.

Now she stops. Stops talking, stops trying to control, to spin, to manage. Crumples to the sofa, sobbing. It's disorienting, and drives the spike of loss deeper into my bones.

Eventually, Artie speaks the words again as I think them.

"We have to call Livie."

Speed makes a noise, but he brings my phone over to the couch. He perches behind us, touching our shoulders.

"I can talk to her," Artie says as I stare at the number without hitting Send.

"It'll take both of us," I say.

"What time is it in Georgia?" Speed asks.

"It's the morning," Artie says.

"It doesn't matter what time it is." I push the button. It rings.

"Hello?" Tyler's young man's voice cracks on the *lo?*

"Ty . . . " My voice is flat, carefully neutral. "Is Livie with you?"

"Why? What's wrong?"

Maybe my voice isn't as smooth as I thought.

"Get Livie," I say, and the tremble is there.

"Mom!" Tyler yells, and I can hear him running, doors opening, and then I hear Livie's voice call, "What?"

I hear the large-room hiss as Tyler puts me on speaker.

"It's Rox," Ty says, and his use of my childhood nickname, the one from Joshua, wrings the sob from my throat.

"Is everything all right?" Livie says.

The words spill out of me like poison filling a clear reservoir.

"I'm so sorry. There's been an accident. Or maybe not an accident. We don't know." Then I lose the words, my voice frozen.

Artie takes a deep breath and reaches for my phone. "Livie, it's me. Joshua seems to have gone swimming in the middle of the night. He never came back. We have the Coast Guard searching for his b—for him. It's not looking good."

Ty sobs a choking cry for his big brother. Livie is less sentimental. She almost sounds angry.

"What do you mean, 'not looking good'? Where the hell is he?"

"We don't know," Artie says. "It's been hours with no sign."

"That's not possible." Livie is not ready for this news. None of us is.

"Livie . . ." Artie says. "I'm sorry. We're all just so . . ."

And then it sinks in across the miles. A howl pierces the air. Livie.

Artie murmurs comfort, then takes control.

"I'll have travel arrangements made. I'll send an assistant to help you with packing, with anything you need. Should I have Dr. Matt send a prescription?"

I want to scream at her, but the urge is split inside me, separate from how we are united now, facing this horror. This loss.

We're crying, we're planning, we're trying to handle it.

Artie speaks the words, becomes the captain of our capsized world. Artie will arrange everything.

Then she's done talking and the phone is back in my hand. I crawl back onto the sofa, pull Speed with me.

We huddle under a blanket together, holding each other like little kids pretending the world cannot see us. The phone is clamped to my ear.

I'm off speakerphone. It's just me and Tyler.

Crying with each other, long distance made hideously close.

And then I'm off the phone and Speed is holding me, both of us crying without words. In my mind, I hear Joshua, can't stop hearing Joshua.

I'm sorry for everything.

Anger lashes through me. I can't believe he would kill himself. But if he didn't—

Then it was as if he knew something might happen. A pervading sense of doom that he lived with, couldn't shake. Ever since Dallas, maybe even before that. Ever since he couldn't be anyone other than *Joshua Blackbird*.

But the towel. He meant to come back. Didn't he? He wouldn't do that to us. He wouldn't do that to *me.*

He loved me too much to hurt me like that.

Was he scared? When he started to flounder? When he got a cramp or when he realized he had gone too far?

When he realized he was drowning?

My mind has become the security footage, playing back and playing back. The moment when Joshua sat at the top of the ladder. When he went into the water. When he floated on his back, feet hooked in the ladder.

When he swam away from the light.

14

ALTERNATE UNIVERSE

Twelve hours later, the Coast Guard officially changed their mission from "search and rescue" to "recovery." Joshua Blackbird was presumed dead.

Then he was declared dead.

Time warped, stretching and shrinking, not for a moment feeling real. Days passed in a surreal blur.

There was a good-bye, a memorial service at a cemetery, even though we had nothing to bury. There was a stone, a plaque would arrive later. All of it happened there in LA. The loss was everywhere, and so were the reporters. The television stations, the journalists, and bloggers. Birdies across the globe held vigils—an outpouring of loss.

How can you pour out your loss?

If I could pour out loss, I would. I would allow it to

gather and spill, like grains of sand, always more, an ocean of it, corrupted sediment that wrenches up and out, continuously.

In LA we moved carefully around each other. Livie was all red eyes and dazed wandering through the mansion. Tears and talk of heaven.

Ty would hover on the edge of a room if I was in it, waiting for me to see him before he came in. Surprising me every time with his new height, even as he slouched. With his young man's broadening shoulders.

Even though he's only a year younger than me, I still can't help thinking of him as Joshua's pesky kid brother.

We all look older now, I guess. Carrying the weight of loss in our faces and bodies.

But under Ty's grief I could still see the sun-bleached ease of his life before *Joshua Blackbird*. Another boy from Marchant.

That helped me talk to him, late nights in the mansion kitchen, when we couldn't escape our loss, even in sleep, because he was *not* like his brother in so many ways.

Ty was certain, completely certain, that Joshua's death was accidental. Our late-night conversations were a tiny echo of the wider world, where debate raged online, on Twitter, on Tumblr, and on gossip sites and shows.

Was it suicide? In that column put the seeming farewell of "Orpheus's Last Lyric." Add the numerous reported struggles. The breakdowns. The stalker attack. The pressure. The fame. The largesse with his money—was he trying to send a signal? His father's death. A family history of depression.

Was it an accident? In that column add the towel. The careful placement of his shirt over his phone. Both resting as if Joshua meant to pick them up again. Meant to climb out of the water and dry off. Add to that the happy kid's smile, anticipating a swim. Add everything he had, everyone who loved him. A sold-out tour, the world his for the asking.

Add to either column his other depressive or obscure lyrics before they were reworked by other writers into more marketable *Joshua Blackbird* songs. In one column, these lyrics showed a pattern of depression; in the other, the growth of an artist learning his aesthetic. Which made "Orpheus's Last Lyric" part of a larger shift of work, not a singular farewell.

Tyler's voice remained calm, even as he heard my doubts. Even as he heard the damning arguments that showed Joshua's death could have been suicide.

He is still steadfast in his certainty that it was an accident. I want to believe that with everything that is in me. I want to believe it with every breath.

I don't want to wake up in the middle of the night, every night, wondering what I didn't do that I could have. That I should have.

Angel Rey came and cried with us. Real tears, not for any cameras. Before and after the memorial service. That day, vivid and unreal. A private ceremony, but the Birdies were there, lining the road between the chapel and the cemetery. Silent and crying, holding flowers, throwing the flowers at the limos, since there was no hearse, gripping giant pictures with his heartbreak smile.

The blur of shared time lost, of grief spent together, continued for some time after the service.

We came together as a group one final time and filmed a public service announcement.

It was Tyler's idea. He knew that there were fans who believed their favorite musician had committed suicide.

He couldn't stand the thought that it would be something they would think of as a choice. Or that they might see as romantic. A grand gesture. A way out. The only way.

Tyler's wide-open heart drove him, coaxing Artie to help him set up the Blackbird Foundation, a crisis intervention group, rooted in fandom, seeking to empower and aid anyone who needed it.

They interviewed and hired foundation members and employees, basing it in LA. Using an empty office in the suite Joshua had bought for Artie as the headquarters.

Even Artie was completely on board in the end.

The primary message was one of hope. That depression lies. That no one is alone; there is help. For everyone.

Even if I didn't share Ty's conviction that Joshua's death was an accident, I shared his goal—that the message was important and people needed to hear it.

And it helped everyone, I think, to say something. To take action.

To try to build a safety net to catch others when the one we lost had slipped past us ever more steadily into the dark.

Then after that, however slowly, life moved on. People moved on.

Livie and Tyler went back to Georgia.

And I went with them, home to Marchant. To Grandma, who wanted to share my grief but couldn't travel to LA. So I packed up my few mementos, my circus books, a few of Joshua's shirts that still smelled like him, my clothes, and the tablet.

Before we left, Artie sat us down. For once she seemed to be having a hard time talking but eventually got through what she was trying to say.

When Joshua turned seventeen and emancipated himself just a few months ago, when he took control of all his assets, separating them from Livie, he met with some financial advisors.

In addition to setting up Livie's allowance and a fund for Ty's schooling, he had drawn up a will.

It would take a little while to get sorted out, but we

were all taken care of. Ty, Livie, me. Santiago and Speed and the rest of the band. Even Artie.

Joshua had also arranged for the dancers and roadies to be paid for a year's worth of work should the tour be cancelled for any reason.

Somehow I made myself sit quietly and listen. Held my mouth clamped shut and didn't turn to Ty and howl that this was the ultimate proof that Joshua had taken his own life.

He had left no question of where his money would go.

But Ty asked the question anyway, in the middle of it, asked Artie if she knew why his brother had done this thing. The will. The accounts.

Artie shrugged and said he had wanted everything done at once when he was emancipated. So he wouldn't have to think of it again. A single blur of lawyers, papers, and signings.

So we all had a little money now. Gifts from Joshua with which we could do whatever we wanted.

In the exhaustion of numbed grief, it felt like another grudge I would carry against Joshua. An anger I would inhabit later, when I had the emotional strength to feel it. That he would think of everyone around him, that he would give to each of us, yet didn't care enough about himself—or me—to wake me up so that he wouldn't be swimming in the middle of the night all alone, in an ocean so large that it could swallow lives whole, gone without a trace.

I came home to my grandma's, and now it's almost as if I never left. Except the house is new, modest but new, nice. Not a trailer. A ranch style, brick and siding and shutters, a wide front porch with rockers. Four bedrooms for two of us, plenty of room to go and be by myself if I need to.

Mostly I follow Grandma around like a satellite. Following her daily, elderly person schedule. One foot in front of the other in a daze of deliberately suppressed feeling.

I won't listen to the radio with her, so we watch daytime TV, napping with it on, with lunch uneaten or half-eaten. Every day empty, every day the same. I only leave the house to take Grandma to her doctor in town. Or I'll drive us to the grocery store, and I don't even shoplift anything to make it fun. I'll take her in, help her get the things on her list.

Sometimes we'll go into the army surplus store and the string of pawnshops and thrift stores across from the Dollar General. I'll buy thick canvas army belts with flat brass snap buckles, or surplus desert boots, or black BDU pants. Anything that feels like it was supposed to be somewhere else, doing something important.

Saving somebody.

I cut them off or tear them up, or draw on them with marker, hitching belts and buckles tight over my waist and hips, wearing them with secondhand shirts from bands people once loved.

I nearly shave my head, but in the end just hack at it with scissors like I always do, dumping a whole bottle of insane red over it when it starts to grow out too much.

I read all my books again. Lose myself in them like losing myself in a pillow fort.

I reread everything about Lillian Leitzel. All the circus books I have, piecing her story together. She would pin her long hair up in sections, so that as she twirled and lunged it would fall down, piece by piece, like she was an engine revving, shaking itself apart with the violence of her abilities.

I sprawl in my bed, reading all the different retellings of her tragedy, and the tangled tragedies that came after. A harrowing story of untimely deaths, first accidental, then deliberate. And before death, the sorrowful tale of lovers who couldn't be together, despite their passion. Or perhaps because of it. How the love of her life, her estranged husband, Alfredo Codona, spiraled into slow, desolate self-destruction from the loss of her. Even though they were separated when she fell, even though they had fought viciously when together and after separating Codona pursued another; still their love consumed them, refusing to be extinguished. They had been trying to come together again. When she fell, he raced to her side.

She died two days later.

In the end, Codona's grief became destructive. It started a downward curl of despair. He took death-courting risks on the trapeze; threw endless, dangerous tricks Leitzel had forbidden him from performing. Without her, no one told him no. No one could catch his endless falling. He threw himself away, ruined his shoulder, and could no longer perform at all. He married again, another circus performer, Vera Bruce, even though he knew she didn't love him. Even though he still loved Leitzel.

Perhaps the choice to marry Vera was just more falling, or perhaps it was a desperate grab at a chance at love and life again, even as he fell out of control, down and down, his story ultimately ending when he left the circus completely, and Vera left him. When she filed for divorce, something snapped in him, some last safety catch that linked him to who he used to be. He killed her and then himself, made himself a murderer, a twisted thing that once had been the King of the Trapeze.

Losses warped him, first the loss of Leitzel, then the loss of his abilities, and finally the loss of how he saw himself. He became a broken, tragic, and hateful creature.

But Leitzel . . .

Leitzel was always a blazing fire, true to herself. Passionate where others were timid, risking everything for a single moment of love and the adoration of the crowd.

It unfurls as I read, the reason I have always been in love with her, my Lillian Leitzel, the Queen of the Air. With my idea of her. Her life, a little like Joshua's, nothing like mine, except for the hunger that was never sated.

It's her passion for life that I love. Her daring. How she would claw and fight for what she wanted, fearless and unashamed, drinking life in great, sloppy drafts, never once slowing or counting the cost.

She makes me feel brave even though she fell. Because she risked falling.

I can let go of the bar, can let myself fall through the air. It doesn't matter if the ground is rushing up toward me, or if there is a net waiting to catch me. It doesn't matter if no one else sees me fall. The point is to fly, even for a second.

I start lurking in online Birdie chats, follow them on Tumblr, on Twitter, search all the blogs and forums and hashtags I can find.

Holding on to Joshua through them.

There's a bloom of fan-edit videos every week, memorials, GIFs of tribute flowers and his perfect, shattering smile.

Then there's footage from the last concert.

The whole thing is getting released, first streaming on a paid site, then on Blu-ray and across all platforms, *The Last Concert*. The show interspersed with interviews with the band.

Interviews with Angel Rey and Speed, both seeming shell-shocked with loss.

Artie's on it as well, talking about Joshua Blackbird's *legacy*. As if she is the one to protect it for the ages. As if he were entirely her doing.

More time passes.

"Forever or Never" is everywhere. Every radio station, Pandora, YouTube, hits that keep ratcheting up, bookending a public life, just the way it started.

A death benefit. It would have been a hit anyway. Of course it would. Look at him singing it on *The Late Late Show*. It's searing. Like a wound opening. The troubled eyes, the strangely haunted yet energized lyrics.

The Birdies love it, cry over it, comment on it. They make art from his art. Tributes, videos, drawings. Detune the song and slow it down. Make his song plaintive and sorrowful.

I even find a beautiful, hand-drawn pencil sketch of a photo Artie stole from my phone and used as the cover art for the single "Lullaby for Love."

It feels like a punch that takes my air, and I can't stop looking at it.

There are all-out fandom wars between Birdies who think Joshua committed suicide and Birdies who think his death was accidental. Their battles flame across channels, across Twitter and Tumblr and fan-fiction sites, scouring each other with their certainty.

Birdies who want to grieve and don't want to pick sides tag their posts with #DovesForLove.

There are even Birdies who are convinced Joshua isn't dead at all: #LazarusBirds. Their theories are ink-black poison to me, dumping pain into my veins. The death deniers uniformly sound like the type of conspiracy theorists who think the moon landing was faked, or that Tupac is still alive.

I filter and block them out every time I'm online. There are only a few of them, the smallest subset, and it's easy to make it to where I don't ingest their poison.

I create a sock-puppet account, a fellow-Birdie profile, to join in their obsessive fascinations. To talk about the moment in "Forever or Never" at 2:26 when his voice cracks, real emotion, not performance—

I start reading fanfics, RPF—Real Person Fics. I even find myself in a few of them. The Girl from Home.

I know it's unhealthy. I don't care.

I devour them. All of them. I read the ones where he's with Angel Rey. I read the ones where he's with an OFC (Original Female Character) or OMC (Original Male Character). I read the ones where he's with Speed or other guys from the band, other celebrities, the opening act. I read the ones where he's with Tyler.

Weeks pass as I live in the stories they weave for me.

It's a sickness that I cannot purge. It's a sickness, and I let it take root.

I feed it.

I read alternate universe adventures where we all live in a medieval world with dragons, or have superpowers and fight crime. I read the "five times" story prompts, read the requests for "fix-it" fics, where everything is magically made better.

I read about imagined first times that never were: first loves, first kisses. It makes it safe, cushioned in the haze of fiction, to think of what actually happened. Real moments, beautiful and worth remembering.

The first time Joshua kissed me, we were in the ninth grade. It was by the lake, this little inlet, a bubble of water that seeped into a kidney-shaped area where there was a free boat launch that the power company maintained. Even though most of the people who went there didn't have boats and just used the ramp as a zero-entry walkway into the lake.

Years ago, some kids had found a ski towrope floating on the water, tangled in the tree stumps and leaf-stir, shallow grass, and other debris, thrown off or snapped or otherwise just lost from the fast boats that fly by in the middle of the lake, a world away from us clinging to the edges.

The towrope had then been tied to a leaning tree overhanging the water's edge. If you could climb at all, you could shimmy up the scrawny, precarious tree, snag the towrope, and pull it back to shore. Kids would spend all summer grabbing the tow bar, swinging out over the water, doing elaborate flips or just letting go, arc-falling sloppy parabolas all the way into the water.

A few kids had been there when we'd first arrived that day, but they'd gone. Ty wasn't with us, either, for a change.

Joshua and I swam, splashing each other, floating on our backs, holding on to arms or hands like otters so we wouldn't drift away from each other.

We were floating. The water tipped over my stomach when I moved my legs to stay afloat. Joshua rolled at me and pushed me down, dunking me, then wrapped his arm around my back, pulling me back up.

I dunked him in revenge and took off, swimming as fast as I could to the shore.

Joshua followed and then forgot about revenge, focused on climbing the tree to get the towrope.

When he had it, he shimmied down the tree and held it out to me.

"You can have it first."

"Thanks." I grabbed the tow bar and planted my feet on the worn root-shelf, leaning back, most of my weight borne by the ski rope.

But Joshua was still holding on to the bar, standing beside me, near the slope-leaning tree, a small smile on his lips.

My heart stuttered, unable to decide how to react,

speed up or slow down, as Shu leaned into me, touching his lips to mine.

He held on to the ski bar with one hand and slid the other around my shoulders, like he could keep me from falling, both of us letting our weight pull against the towrope.

His lips were soft and warm, and neither of us closed our eyes.

Then he was straightening, an even bigger smile on his face. He let go of the tow bar, leaving it in my hands.

"Okay," he said, sweeping a hand toward the lake. "Have a nice flight."

I jumped up and back, pulling myself up on the bar, swinging out over the water. Letting go at the right moment, at the height of the arc, you could feel like you might take to the air, for a single instant.

I yelled and threw my arms out, pinwheeling to stay upright, running my legs, a holler of exhilaration, cut off when I submerged in the water.

Joshua grabbed the rope and swung, doing a belly-curled horse-dive, hitting the water with just the right concussive force that it whumped as the air was pushed down and out, showering me.

A memory that takes my breath away, that comforts and cuts. So I lose myself online again, in the fandom, a filter between me and grief.

The best things, better than the videos, the fics, the

GIFs—the best of them all, are the accounts devoted to decoding "Orpheus's Last Lyric."

Which is being recorded, of course. For the tribute album.

The entertainment news shows and the gossip bloggers had already swarmed over the lyrics, especially the title, reporting about the myth of Orpheus, a demigod with a divine voice that could enchant any listeners. Who moved even the beasts and the rocks with his songs. He fell in love with Eurydice, and when she died, went into the underworld to bring her back, but failed. Orpheus mourned and sang his grief. He died, torn to pieces by the wild women, the Maenads, who could not stand that he would not love them.

The talking heads draw parallels to the Birdies, to the frenzy of "fangirls," and especially to Mira, of course.

But the Birdies dig deeper. They analyze the lyrics. Illustrate each line with pictures, video clips, links to supplemental material, interviews, poems, texts—

And for all their fanatical devotion, for all that people have always derided the enthusiasm of young women, of "fangirls," for all the ways the world—myself included—mocks them—

They're *not stupid.*

I read their analyses. Because I will never know what he meant, and I can never ask him. So I feed from the hive mind of the Birdies. For them it's purging. For me it's oxygen, water.

JoshuaMyLove posted a link to a poem on the National Poetry Foundation website—one I remember reading with Ms. Kearney and Joshua, back before the tour began.

JoshuaMyLove: "Orpheus's Last Lyric" References This Poem—"Not Waving but Drowning" by Stevie Smith.

Hits and reblogs and comments follow.

The title of the poem. The one he quoted in "Orpheus's Last Lyric." That talks about drowning.

The whole line is from the dead man—the poem, short and devastating, starts like it's being told. A story. A sad thing that happened.

And that was what I remember affected Joshua when we studied it.

"They don't even *know* him," he had said, finger jabbing at the text. Ms. Kearney had waited for him to say more, his participation rare, his engagement virtually extinct.

I waited, too.

"They're talking about him, how he liked to play jokes, I guess," he had said.

Ms. Kearney nodded.

"They didn't even know. They didn't have a clue what was really happening. Not just with the drowning—but all of it. He was just—*this guy*. He was just this role to them."

And then we talked about that. About perception and narrative in poetry. About loss and the difficulty of being vulnerable, of asking for help. Of being authentic, or trying for authenticity.

All these elevated concepts, camouflaging a genuine struggle.

Like all we were talking about was that damn poem. Because no one wanted to say what we were really talking about.

The grind of the machine.

Being *Joshua Blackbird.*

Time continues to stumble by.

"You need to get out," Grandma says. "Get out of the house. Go for a walk. Anything."

"You too, then," I say.

She hardly ever leaves the house. It's a whole big scary sky out there, and she has to pull her oxygen tank everywhere.

Grandma frowns at me. "I'll get my coat," she says.

I suppose that's love.

I yank on black tac pants and peg them over my Docs. Pull on a ripped T-shirt and knot it at my waist.

We walk to the end of the driveway and back. It doesn't change anything.

Back inside the house, Grandma falls back into her chair.

"Good work," I say. "We did a lot today."

"Smart alec," she snaps. "Get out of my house and don't come back until you've broken a sweat."

I walk back outside.

The setting sun casts a golden glow across the dead grass. It feels a little warm but mostly ineffectual, like words on a condolence card.

But it feels good, being outside. For some stupidly pointless reason. I sit on the dead grass, feeling the cool of the earth through the stiff black pants. I lie back, stretching my arms out, the prickling of the grass along my bare arms like the scratching of a memory, tugging at your attention.

The ground is cold. The earth is dark and deep. Or something like that. A line from another poem.

What the hell with all the poems? Every poem Ms. Kearney tried to teach us. Why are they all coming back to me now?

I swipe at my cheeks and get up. Start walking. Fast, up the driveway, down the cul-de-sac, down the road. When I'm not looking at the computer, at the BlueBirdie blogs, the world is too present—I'm too alone—and—

Everything's too real.

My phone vibrates.

Tyler. His daily attempt to reach me. He'll be expecting my voice mail—my daily refusal to be reached.

"Hey," I answer. *Surprise.*

"Hey! Roxy!" he says back. And he doesn't sound mad that I haven't been answering the phone these past months. He just sounds—like someone happy to hear my voice.

"Hey, Ty," I say.

He sighs, and then we don't say anything.

"So," he finally says, "Artie sent me a rough cut of the tribute album. And a disc that goes with it—like a featurette. And. I want to watch it. I want to hear it. But—I don't want to. You know?"

I laugh, a dark, sniffling loss-cough. "Yeah. I get it."

I hear the shivery breath he takes. Can picture him, how he does, hunching skinny-wide shoulders, slouching his head low. Trying to stop it. Not being able to.

Trying to need less. Take up less space, be a shadow.

Ty always wanted to be his big brother's shadow. Now there's no one for him . . . certainly not Livie, who was barely there in the best of times.

I glare back up the street at Grandma's house.

"If I start walking now, I should be there in forty minutes," I say, with no real idea how long it will take, but just striking out anyway. It's a goal. It's a destination. It's one step in front of the other.

"Forget that. I'll come pick you up," he says.

"You and your mom? I don't think so."

"Whatever. I'll come get you."

He hangs up.

I shrug and walk back home. I sprawl in the grass again. It's starting to feel a little colder, with the sunlight stealing from the sky.

It takes about fifteen minutes before I hear a high, buzzing engine, so there's no way my walk estimate was even remotely accurate.

Joshua bought his mom one of those ridiculous, giant SUVs that petite women love to drive.

The double-stroke engine whine turns the corner onto my street. And I start to laugh.

Ty is riding his dirt bike.

You can take the boy out of the county, but you can't take the county out of the boy.

He pulls around the dead-end loop and pops the bike out of gear, doing a typical final rev. He's wearing faded farm jeans and a red T-shirt advertising the local dirt track. With his sneakers braced wide, he unhooks a spare helmet from the bungee strap. He doesn't take off his own helmet, black and red with a visor and face mask.

It's disconcerting, seeing only his eyes, so much like Joshua's, staring out at me.

"Here!" he shouts, and lobs the helmet at me.

It's all so country it hurts. But it's also perfect: the sleek black and red, with helmets matching the bike.

Joshua bought it—a whole kit. I remember hearing him talking about it with Ty over the phone.

I remember him telling Ty, "Don't break your neck."

I wonder if he ever even saw the bike or the gear.

Tyler glares at me through the helmet. "Any day, Roxy."

"You're going to double me. You." I'm standing beside him now. It's shocking, actually, how long his legs are, sprawled out to hold the bike.

His eyes narrow. Who is this kid? Ty used to laugh off our teasing, mine and Joshua's.

Before the YouTube video happened, before Artie came, before any of it.

"I'm only a year younger than you," Ty says. "You can drop the wise-old-lady act."

I shrug and mash the helmet on. My fingers poke at the edges of the eye gap, stuffing spiky chunks of hair underneath.

The engine is still running. Ty holds out a surprisingly broad hand to help me lever myself onto the back.

The bike is a narrow muscle, not really made for doubling, but I straddle behind him.

Ty revs an all-clear signal. I grab on to his shoulders, but he pulls out fast enough that I have to clutch at him.

We're a bottle rocket up the street and down the road.

The bike is built like Ty is—all length and angularity. Skinny. No, not skinny. *Lean*—the lean of rawboned growth, of becoming.

The night is growing cold, but I don't feel it riding on the back of Ty's bike. We're weaving through back roads and residential developments, trying to stay off the busier route, since the bike isn't street legal.

It feels good leaving the world behind.

15

A SONG FOR JOSHUA

Ty pulls up to the gate at the bottom of the driveway. There are no Birdies this late at night, and no cameras. His connection to his brother is only as good as the latest news—so until the tribute album officially releases, there won't be much ruckus at the gates.

Although the flowers and cards and little teddy bears still look fresh enough to have been delivered today.

Ty snakes a hand into his coat and then the gate is opening. We zoom up the road and behind the massive house. Really it's a McMansion just like all the others in this part of town, but I can't get past the "mansion" part, because that's what they all are.

"I always forget how big this place is," I say when he cuts the engine.

Ty helps me climb off, then he drops the stand and takes off his helmet.

He glances up at the house. "Yeah. I only use part of it."

He didn't mean to be funny, but I laugh anyway. That reflexive, trailer park takedown before anyone else can do it for you.

"Well, all right. As long as you're only using part," I say.

Ty laughs and takes my helmet. At the back door he punches in the security code and closes the door behind us.

He puts the helmets on a closet shelf.

"Where's Livie?" The house is silent, and big as it is, it feels empty.

"Out. Ladies' night out or a date. I can't remember which."

There's grit in the words.

He turns toward the kitchen. "Let's get some food."

He's not as interested in snacks as he is in plain fuel, so he haphazardly grabs a bag of Doritos, some Oreos, cups with ice, and a two-liter bottle of Coke.

Ty leads the way through an overdecorated sitting room, past a dining room where there are eight sets of china set on the table at the empty seats, gold charger plates, embroidered napkins.

"It must be like living in Barbie's Dreamhouse," I say.

"Pretty much."

We walk into the TV room, and even though it's on the main floor, it feels like Ty's the only one who really spends time here. There are game consoles, the pillow from his bed on the massive sofa, cartridges and cases cluttering surfaces.

A torn padded envelope. I recognize Artie's precise handwriting.

Ty spreads a Mexican blanket on the floor, and we set down the plastic cups, the chips, the cookies, and the Coke bottle.

For some reason we stand there and look at it for a split second.

"All it needs is some beer cans, and it's a redneck wedding reception," Ty says.

We laugh stupidly, a release valve more than humor, and then sit down on the blanket, ignoring the sofa like we're little kids.

Ty sighs and hands me the padded envelope.

I take out the disc, and he puts it in the console. It buzzes up, a professional title card, *Orpheus's Last Lyric: A Tribute to Joshua Blackbird.*

And it's hokey, the background of the menu. Slow-motion sepia-toned footage of Joshua laughing, singing, smiling his heartbreak smile.

Still, it hits me where it hurts.

"Oh." There is a choke of emotion in my throat. "Maybe

this was a bad idea." I down a slug of my drink, trying to wash the emotion away.

Ty swipes at his eyes with a knuckle but doesn't say anything. He hits Play.

It starts, performance videos in a studio. You can already imagine the tribute concert.

Angel Rey is first. Her high, clear voice is like a shiver of crystal. Her version of "Orpheus's Last Lyric" is slow, mournful. A lovesick ballad.

And that makes sense, but it's not *right* either. It's not what he meant.

The first video ends, and next is footage of Joshua performing, one of the first tour dates. He looks so purposeful. So energetic.

I'd forgotten what he could be like.

I don't even notice when the tears start.

I shove jagged chips into my mouth, just to have something to bite.

Then the next tribute is up, Mendicant's Son, one of the opening bands, playing a more dissonant cover of Joshua's "Come Home."

Ty drains his Coke and shoves Oreos into his mouth without interest.

Two more tributes go by, an up-and-coming band I think we met backstage somewhere.

Then there's a final version of "Orpheus's Last Lyric"

by Misplaced. I don't know the band. The production quality is not as high as the others. It seems to be here as an afterthought.

Then I see Speed behind the drum kit. There's Quinn and Stevie.

Joshua's band. For some reason, I wasn't expecting that. It's another thing that's wrong in a series of horrible errors.

It's all surreal, and I've pushed through sorrow to numbness. It's a movie of a tragedy, a history.

Not something recent, not something that happened to me.

I'm not flying . . . I'm falling.

Quinn steps up to the studio mic.

"We just." Quinn waves a hand. "We just wanted to try this. For Joshua. We miss you, brother."

They start playing. It's a lurching calliope rock-sound. It fits better than Angel's dirgelike attempt, but it's meandering.

"I need to call Speed," I say, remembering all the times I dodged his number on the incoming caller ID or returned haphazard, vague texts. Maybe he was trying to tell me about this.

"I need to do lots of things," Ty says.

Then the disc plays a compilation of Joshua performance clips, over the live version of "Forever or Never." The one from opening night.

The night he left us.

I can't look at him, and I can't look away. The perfection of his face. His half smile. Remembering when we lived in Marchant, how he used to double me on his handlebars to go to the lake.

How I used to let him climb in my bedroom window, him and Ty, when Livie would bring a guy home they didn't like.

How natural it was. How easy. How easy it was to be with him—before.

His first guitar sits in the corner of this room, on a stand. Ready, like he might walk in and pick it up. The same guitar he used to play when he'd sing to me.

The numbing insulation is stripped off my grief, and the pain wires spark. They spark.

I catch Ty's eyes. "Yeah," he says. "I know." He stares at a Dorito in his fingers, sends it spinning with a flick. There's something angry about the gesture.

The disc starts playing at the beginning again. Angel Rey's dirge.

"What a bunch of crap," Ty says.

"She's nice."

"Sure, but her version sucks."

"It all sucks."

Ty glances at me, and in his eyes I see a lurking secret.

"What?"

Ty shrugs, like *no big deal.*

I let my eyes sit on him till he cracks.

"I . . . well . . . I been playing with a version," he says.

He says it like it's shameful.

It makes perfect sense. While I've been obsessed with figuring out the lyrics and studying the BlueBirdies, he's been noodling with the guitar, Joshua's first, and trying to fit his brother's words to music.

Each of us wrestling with it.

I cross my arms and glare at the guitar on the stand.

Ty's shoulders bunch as he scrubs his head.

"Why not," he says.

I push myself off the floor and curl into the couch. Prop against Ty's pillow.

Ty gets the guitar.

And it's like déjà vu. That guitar, and how Ty becomes this new person when he slings the strap across his shoulders.

Suddenly his awkward height becomes a presence. The habitual slouch becomes a guitarist's pose.

Ty fiddles with the knobs, tuning the strings. Getting the sound just right. Then he strums out a series of chords, a heavy rock-blues sound. Ty strikes the strings, slapping and thumping the wood for a percussive kick.

He lifts his jaw and closes his eyes, starts to sing.

His voice is nothing like Joshua's. No range, no distinct

sound. Just a raw voice, his words sung like they're pressed out from behind clenched teeth.

When he gets to the chorus, his voice breaks.

It's exactly perfect. The grated sound, the unartfulness of it, the dirty broken-down blues riff that rocks harder and harder at each chorus. Ty's voice is an instrument of grit.

His rendition packs an emotion more fitting for the Last Lyric. Distortion: sustained, dropped. Each string torqued for the wrung-out note.

He takes a guitar solo bridge, then lets that energy feed into the last lines of the song.

And then silence. The only sound the echo of the notes.

"That was perfect," I say.

His eyes, downcast, can't meet mine. He looks uncomfortable as he lifts the guitar strap from around his head, sets the instrument back on its stand. Like he got caught doing something he wasn't supposed to. He's back to being awkward Ty, all loose limbs and jagged movements.

And then, because he sang to me, I tell him about the BlueBirdie blogs. And the Tumblrs. And the real-person fics. And every unhealthy way I've tried to bury myself in it.

With Joshua.

Ty gets his tablet, and we're looking at the poems, and we're talking about "Orpheus's Last Lyric," and what it means. And I see it clearly now.

There's a brooding undercurrent in Joshua's words, beneath the apologies. A self-destructive loathing—which is why none of the other versions of "Orpheus's Last Lyric" on the tribute album work. In fact, it's why they're all wrong.

It's not pop music at all. Only one person understood that.

"Your version is the one," I say. "That's the one everyone should hear."

Ty tries to hide his smile. "Yeah?" he says.

"Yeah. Why not? Ty, it's good."

"Thanks. Artie said Angel's would be the first single."

"Figures."

We look on YouTube, because if there's one thing we know about Artie, it's that the woman does not let grass grow under her feet, and if Ty got the screener today . . .

And there it is. Angel's version, already "leaked." Typical. An early, buzz-build move.

For once I don't want to read the comments.

"I want to hear your version again," I say.

"Seriously?"

"Yeah, seriously. Humor me."

"Okay." Ty picks up the guitar, eases the strap back over his head.

"Can I film it on my phone?"

"Why not?" Ty smiles at me and doesn't bother hiding

this one. It's that open smile, so much more carefree than his brother's.

I press Record on my phone.

"This is for my brother," Ty says into the lens.

I'm propped on the sofa to steady my recording. Ty fingers the strings of his dead brother's first guitar. He plays "Orpheus's Last Lyric," and I film it.

It's just as good the second time around.

As the last chord fades into silence, I don't hit Stop, just keep filming as Ty stands there, statue still, waiting in the moment, like the fading note will magic something for him as the song ends.

The he drops his head, floppy dark blond hair curtain-falling into his eyes.

That's when I stop.

Ty returns the guitar to its stand. "We should put it online. Just for us. So I can refine it later." Ty falls onto the sofa near my feet. "I'll set it for private."

I watch the video play.

"It's really good, Ty." Now I'm smiling.

He's good, and he's pure, and he's Shu's kid brother.

But he's his own person, only a year younger than me. Sixteen, only just. His birthday fell when I was ignoring him, ignoring everyone.

"Put it online," Ty says, lifting his head, looking at me. "I just don't want her version to be what everyone thinks of as 'Orpheus's Last Lyric.'" He shakes his head. "Not that mine is, but hers . . ."

"I get it, Ty. I really do. Let's post it."

Ty sits up. I give him my phone and scoot beside him, watching as he logs in to his YouTube account and loads it.

"It's not like I have any followers or anything," Ty says. "I'm on there as BikeRTy. Just a few people will see it, maybe. I mostly post dirt track videos." He shrugs.

"Ty, it's cool. I need it to be there, too."

"Okay."

It doesn't matter who sees it. Or who *doesn't*. We know we did it. That's all.

I finally feel good about something.

16

DESPERATE OR WANTING

I get some Oreos, and Ty changes out the disc for some superhero movie. All bashes and crashes and cities being destroyed.

I'm not really watching. It's late and I close my eyes. My head must loll sideways on the back of the couch, because I jerk it up, feeling for an instant like I'm falling.

"So graceful," Ty teases. Then he slides closer and guides my head onto his shoulder. "Here."

I stay there. It's not uncomfortable, and it's easy to just slip into and out of sleeping, opening and closing my eyes as the movie goes on without me.

I don't realize that we're both sleeping until we topple sideways on the sofa.

I land on Ty's side, along his ribs and arms, as his head whumps onto the sofa cushion.

"Whoops," I say.

Ty shifts, rolling fully onto his back on the sofa. He gently pulls his arm out from under me as he moves slightly away. Hair is sticking up on one side of his head.

He smiles and suddenly looks bashful. That smile, all innocence and open heart. His eyes when they find mine look like Joshua's, the same shape, the same color, but no shifting shadows inside, no sleepless smudges beneath. Ty's eyes smile at me, and I see the emotion in them like it's words written on the page.

His fingers brush softly up my arm.

I feel my breath catch.

This is not the Ty I remember.

But I'm not the same girl who grew up with him, but never really saw him. Who left when everything changed.

And that's when *he* changed. Grew up.

It's a time-stop moment. A breath-hold moment, the time stretch, two points coming together—the paper folding back on itself—

The moment before, and the moment after.

I am almost frozen as well, except I'm breathing faster than I was. Without closing my eyes, I move my face closer to his.

My fingers slide over his cheek and through the sandy hair behind his ear before pulling behind the curve of his neck.

With my eyes open, I watch as he obeys my hand, lifting his lips to mine.

We look at each other.

His lips are chapped and hesitant. They meet mine, but slowly, like a butterfly landing.

It makes me angry. I do not want to be kissed gently.

It's not wrong, that I'm kissing him, but it's not romance. It may not ever be simple when we kiss, but it isn't impure. And it's not this fragile thing, either.

So I press my lips hard, feeling his give. I open my mouth and press in—my teeth click against his.

He's still frozen, except now he's kissing me back.

My tongue sweeps into his mouth as I reposition myself over him, lifting to be able to reach him better.

Ty's hands grab my upper arms, closing and urging, so I straddle him. Pull with the hand behind his head. Our teeth click again, but he's doing what I want.

He sits up under me, arms reaching around my back. I keep my hold on his head, pulling his mouth into mine as he strokes a hand up my back and into my hair.

His lips are trying to go soft again, his hands slowing.

I make an impatient sound, so he can hear, and press my firm lips into his too-soft ones.

He's a fire under my skin, a roar of noise and urge.

Nothing else matters. Not who I am, not who he was, and not—

I freeze, still pressed to him but motionless, my brain a storm of confusion and anxiety.

I pull back, because what do I even know about what I want?

What about Ty? Here I am, mauling him, because I don't want to feel.

What does he want?

"Rox?" Ty looks up at me, hands still on my back and under my hair. Then they lift slightly.

"It's okay," I say. "I'm sorry."

He watches my face for a moment, and I don't know what to do with my eyes. Don't know what to do with how they fill with tears.

"I'm okay, too." Ty's words, wry, but true.

"I'm sorry," I say again, uselessly, brushing my index finger under my eyelashes. He's searching my eyes like he's looking for something there.

"Don't be sorry," he says. "I'm not."

He leans in slowly, and this time I close my eyes. When we kiss again, it's good, hungry and slow, but not soft, and not demanding, just wanting.

Maybe we can be this for each other, together becoming something, anything, other than who we are when we are alone.

We kiss and touch, gently, for a long while, and then we stop, not moving past this first step, this first place of more-than-friends.

Ty lifts his head from my shoulder and smiles up at me. He yawns and then nudges me off the sofa onto the floor. Ty reaches over me to snag the blanket and throws it over us. He stretches again and gets his pillow.

We huddle together, sharing the pillow and blanket.

We stare into each other's eyes, shy, like a glance could speak.

"I guess that wasn't a good idea?" Ty says, but his expression says differently.

"I don't know that it was an idea at all," I answer, giving us absolution in truth.

Ty smiles at me, that open-sky smile.

"Let's make a deal." He smooths light fingers over my hair. "Let's not think about any of it."

I can't help but laugh. "Sure. Make it a trend."

Ty doesn't laugh. "I'm serious." He drops his hand off me and rolls onto his back. "Can we just not think about it? Just . . . I don't know, enjoy it?"

I can't tell if he is trying to hold on to what happened and is afraid of me killing it.

Or if he's afraid of judging himself.

"Okay," I say. "Hey. Yeah. Let's not think about it." I touch his forearm.

"Good." He doesn't open his eyes as he lifts the arm, an invitation for me to rest against his chest. "Let's get some sleep, then. I'm wiped."

"Good plan," I say. But I can't put my head there, on his chest, like how I used to—

I push his arm down and curl next to him, putting my chin on the top of his shoulder. I drape an arm over his, across his stomach, and squeeze.

We fall asleep with the blanket over us and the TV on.

If Livie comes home, I don't hear her. And under the blanket, if she saw me at all, she'd just see a girl, not me.

Which is true, in a way.

In the morning, even though we made a deal, I can't help thinking about it. Ty's holding on to me, with us like spoons. His arm is wrapped around my middle.

It's hot and too bright in the room. I creep out from under his arm and try to sweep the chip bits back into the empty bag, gather the trash, and look around for a trash can.

"Hey." Tyler watches me from the floor. His face is open and relaxed.

I slip a smile on, but it feels rigid.

The corners of his mouth drop slightly when he sees it.

"Hey," I say. "Morning." I wave a hand at the windows where the sun shines in, like a cop's flashlight.

"You hungry?" Ty stands. "I could make toaster waffles. Or there's cereal."

He looks older, looks my age, until he smiles.

"Yeah, but I should get home. Grandma might worry."

Ty's eyes cut to me. But he doesn't call me on it. How Grandma generally can't keep track of a cat, much less me.

How Grandma let me leave school and go on tour with my boyfriend.

"Okay," he says.

We pull our shoes on in silence. I peg the legs of my tac pants over my Docs.

Ty reaches into the coat closet and hands me the spare helmet.

"Ty, I'm sorry—" I start.

"No harm, no foul. I'm not thinking about it," he says. Even though he doesn't look into my eyes. Even though I can see how hard he's gripping his helmet.

He yanks the back door open. We walk down the porch steps and climb onto the dirt bike.

He jumps on the starter, revving with his wrist while the bike is out of gear. I climb on and grab on to his stomach, clutching tight as he drops into gear, the rear tire sliding and leaving a streak on the driveway.

The bike shoots around the front of the house, where the driveway curves in a semicircle to the front door.

It's then we see the black limousine.

And Artie, impatiently waving off the chauffer's hand

as she climbs out. Her hair perfect, her suit severe, her stilettos red-soled.

She hears us when we see her. Ty skids to a stop, throwing out both legs to hold us.

Artie says something into the phone clamped to her head and turns to us. She stalks over, and it's like a strange dream—how she's here—unannounced—and for a split second I think, *They've found him. Joshua's alive. Of course he is, since I just made out with his little brother, this isn't real, it's fan fiction, and so of course* now *they find him—he was in a coma and now—*

The voice in my head jabbers incessantly, even though I know it's not true—even though I can see that Artie is frowning, even though I can see that she's *furious.*

I still feel it, the chattering voice inside me feels it, like a punch in the chest, the zombie death of that stupid, irrational hope.

"Cut that thing off!" Artie yells at Ty.

Ty cuts the engine and pulls his helmet off. I take mine off too.

Artie isn't surprised it's me. Just stabs a finger at both of us, each phrase its own separate statement.

"What," she says, through gritted teeth. "The hell. Were you. Thinking."

17

THE JOSHUA BLACKBIRD EXPERIENCE

Someone found Ty's version of "Orpheus's Last Lyric."

Then over a million more people found it. In about two hours, Ty's YouTube video had gone viral.

Since she'd negotiated the tribute artist deal, and since Artie was the executor of the Joshua Blackbird Estate, and just because she was Artie, she was pissed.

Unless Ty was willing to record his version for the tribute album. If he'd get into a studio tomorrow, the day after, *but it better be soon or so help me . . .*

"Do you think anyone will even buy the album I put together? Not with Joshua's brother's version out there!"

Artie paces in Livie's dream mansion.

Livie sits on the sofa, chewing on her nails. Livie and I for once exchange the same shell-shocked expressions.

Déjà vu. This is how it started with Joshua, more or less.

Ty looks as shocked as we do, but he doesn't look as scared. Instead he cuts one of those sky-wide smiles at me. I see knowledge in his glance. An emotion I can't name.

Satisfaction, a *we did it!* exultation in his gaze. No matter what happens next, no matter that Artie is trying to shove him on a life-changing roller coaster, all he sees is *the message got out.* Joshua's words, as much as we could understand them.

I can't help but smile back at him for the collusion of this accident, this fated song.

Ty's tribute.

"What are you two idiots smiling about?" Artie snaps. "You should have *called me*. Forget that—you should have *picked up the phone* when I called you!"

It's then I see the tribute album in a sympathetic light. Artie's coping mechanism. I had the Internet, the Birdies, and the fics.

Ty had working on the song. Trying to find a sound for it, his brother's words and his own grief.

Artie had putting the tribute album together.

Artie falls into a chair. "You should have told me," she says to Ty. "I let Speed's tribute band on. And your version is actually *good*."

"I didn't think anyone would care," Ty says.

Artie starts to laugh, a gentle, jagged sound. "You idiot," she says, but her voice is soft. "You're the little brother of the biggest pop star on the planet. Of course everyone cares. *And* you can sing." Artie waves her hand generously. "I mean, your voice isn't bad."

"Gee, thanks."

"You know what I'm saying."

The inevitable silence every time we think of Joshua and his perfect, inimitable voice. Like he's a silent ghost watching us. Hearing his voice in our heads, every memory that cuts.

"Sorry," Artie finally says. "That was rude of me."

"It's okay," Ty says.

Ty actually wants to do it, and I can't ask him, here in front of the others, if what he wants is the tribute album or something more, because to ask pollutes what Artie is positioning, selling, as a pure motive.

A tribute to his dead brother, the tragic star Joshua Blackbird.

Selling the story.

And I can't help remembering Ty visiting the tour all those times. Visiting during recording the albums. Before Livie came to pick him up and took Ty with her, back home to their new McMansion, and wouldn't let him come visit again.

I remember Ty's face all those times. Glowing with hero worship for his big brother, one thing that never changed.

Ty always looked up to Shu, who looked after him in return.

Then when Joshua became famous, it was as if the whole world saw what Ty already knew: he had the coolest brother there ever was.

Now Ty has his own chance to feel the burn of the spotlight.

By the time Artie leaves, she's booked time in an Atlanta recording studio for Ty to record "Orpheus's Last Lyric."

Ty and I stand in the driveway by the dirt bike, watching as the limousine pulls through the gates, past the few Birdies who stand looking up at the house.

Ty gets on the bike and picks up his helmet.

"How do you feel about it?" I ask.

Ty hands me the spare helmet. It felt like a thing that could be mine, before. Now it just feels like something for someone.

Anyone.

"What are we talking about?" Ty studies the face mask of his helmet as if he will find a diamond lodged in the protective plate.

For a split second, I'm confused. The hesitation is damning.

"That's what I thought." Ty pulls his helmet on, and

I can't see his full expression now, except for his eyes, which won't look at me.

"Ty, wait, I was asking about the song, not last night. You said we shouldn't even think—"

The high rev of the dirt bike engine startles me into silence.

Ty still doesn't look at me. He gestures at the bike seat behind him.

I climb on, and I don't know what to do with my hands. I place them at his hips, then lift one to his shoulder.

Ty grabs my floating-for-purchase hand and pulls it around him. He reaches for my other hand and pulls it to the first, leaving his hands over mine, for just a moment.

I'm pressed against his back. He's pulled my hands so tight, I'm hugging him.

He revs the engine, and I squeeze so he knows I'm ready.

He takes off down the driveway, slowing only enough to dart out the opening gate.

A few Birdies scream at him.

Have they seen the video?

If the song keeps blowing up, what will happen? What does Ty want to happen?

We fly through the residential streets and back roads, Ty taking a slightly different route back to Grandma's.

I promise myself I'll think about why he wanted to take a longer drive later.

But then we're there, at my house, and Ty rides up the driveway, skidding to a stop at the top, catching us on his leg.

The front door is open behind the screen. Because it's nearing lunchtime, Grandma thinks it's time to air the house. It's something she always did back when we lived in a tin box on blocks, prop open the door and let out the heat.

Before I can climb off, Ty squeezes my hands again. Then he lets go and leans forward, away from me, putting his hands on the handlebars.

I get off the bike and turn to him. "Ty—"

"We made a deal, Roxy," he says. "Sorry I couldn't stick to it."

Then he revs the engine and accelerates down the driveway, like a rocket leaving the orbit of a planet it hates.

It's been fifteen hours, but I walk back in like it's been five minutes.

Grandma sits in the recliner watching her game shows.

"See?" she says. "I told you it would be good to get out."

18

ACCOMMODATIONS

The next morning, Ty texts me.

Hey, thanks for coming over. Sorry I made it weird.

As if he could make it any weirder than I did, with my kissing him first, with my not letting him kiss me softly in return, with my need to push and pull at him and to lose myself.

Remembering, I want to sink into the mattress, into the carpet under the bed, through the floorboards, into the dirt under the house.

I make myself reply instead. The least I can do.

Are you kidding? I'm the one that made it weird.

Then I send a picture of a puking smiley face.

After a moment, Ty replies, Wanna come to the studio?

I can imagine it, the same studio Joshua went to,

maybe even some of the same session musicians. The same decorations, the same furniture.

The world goes on in repeat.

No thanks. Don't feel so hot.

Pukey face again.

Ty sends a sad face.

I should say something else. I can't think of anything.

Ty does it for me.

Can I come get you when we get back?

A world of hope and a world of *what do I want?*

Finally, I reply. Okay.

Ty sends a wide-open smiley face.

That night we repeat the one before. Ty comes to get me on his dirt bike. We watch TV and play video games. We make out and then fall asleep on the floor.

The rest of the week falls into the pattern. Artie sends a car for Ty every morning. Every morning, it drives him into the city and the studio. Every evening, it drives him back.

Then Ty gets on his dirt bike and comes to get me.

We spend the nights in Ty's TV room. We never go past kissing and touching. It becomes this new thread that we're testing. Seeing if it can be twined into rope, if it will hold us.

We talk about Joshua a few times, but it's not long before we decide, without saying so, that we'll leave the judging to everyone else. Otherwise everything that's happening just feels so overwhelming. We need each other, need to be okay with it.

Joshua is always between us, but more like a bridge than like a wall.

When Ty's version of "Orpheus's Last Lyric" is done, Artie comes by, there's a bunch of papers to be signed.

And it's up to the Internet and the single sales, but by then the YouTube video has quadrupled in views.

Everyone knows what will happen next. The scope of it.

A car takes Ty to the airport. He flies out to LA and performs on a few evening talk shows, although he won't grant interviews.

The pain is still too new, he says. Artie's line, like a script she wrote.

The Birdies eat it up. Ty's song debuts at number one.

But Ty comes back home. Artie loves all of it: the tribute to a big brother, the need to heal at home, the devotion of the Birdies and the strength they offer Ty. Everyone a part of the same story, each playing their role.

Ty keeps coming to get me. Now he has to take a car with a driver, though, for security. An old man with salt-and-pepper hair holds the door for me while Ty waits behind the car's tinted windows.

Artie's edict. Second verse, same as the first. There are to be no pictures of Ty and me together.

One night, Ty comes in a stretch limo. The tribute

album broke records. Ty's version of "Orpheus's Last Lyric" is still a runaway hit—inescapable. So of course, Artie is arranging songwriters, talking with Ty about an album, and Ty is listening.

He plays me his own songs sometimes. He can play some really great delta-bluesy rock, the kind of music Joshua always loved. The kind that Artie and the record label told him to ditch because it wasn't part of the package. "You're too pretty for the blues," Artie told him once. But on Ty the style fits somehow. Maybe because everyone knows he lost his brother . . . or because all of the Birdies are still mourning Joshua, and Ty's undercurrent of sadness speaks to them, makes them feel even more connected to the tragedy and to each other.

Now the limo door opens, and there's Ty standing with an armful of roses and that clear-sky smile.

"Okay?" I say, in my surprise.

Ty gives me the flowers. He's dressed in crisp black jeans and a gray T-shirt. Dressy, compared to his usual farm jeans.

"Thank you—they're beautiful." I carry the bouquet out the door with me, feeling like I must have punched out a beauty queen to be holding this many roses.

Ty takes my hand and tucks it in the crook of his arm. He walks me to the limo, windows tinted blacker than the night.

"What's the occasion?" I ask.

His smile slips, but he puts it back on in an instant. "You'll see."

We climb into the limo. Ty puts up the privacy screen and opens the moonroof. We lean back. The sliver of moon floats over us as the driver cruises on quiet night roads.

Ty takes my hand in his.

"Rox, I know we had a deal."

The nickname his brother gave me jangles in my ears. Suddenly I'm afraid of the next words out of his mouth. I'm not ready to love him in an openhearted way. And I'm not ready to hear him say he loves me.

What we've had has been nice. Needed, even. But I'm still in love with his dead brother.

I will always be in love with Joshua Blackbird.

I freeze, and Ty can feel it.

"It's just," he says, "it's so easy to be with you."

I let out my pent-up breath.

The limo cruises through the night.

"Do you know what today is?" Ty asks.

My mind is blank. It's not his birthday, it's not my birthday, it's not Joshua's birthday. It's a Tuesday, I think, but I can't promise to even know that much.

It's just another day in an endless procession of them.

I can feel the moment stretch as Ty waits. Can feel the moment in his muscles, when he realizes that I have no idea what he's talking about. Can feel it pulling a silent tension into his arms.

The limo, the roses, his clothes.

Has Ty's video of "Orpheus's Last Lyric" hit another ridiculous number?

"I . . ."

Ty lets go of my hand.

"You don't know."

I shake my head. Can't pretend knowledge I don't have.

Ty shifts away from me. The night air is suddenly cool on my side where he had been.

He pushes a button, and the privacy screen lowers.

"Take us home," Ty tells the driver.

We arrive at Livie's McMansion. Birdies shout and press at the limo as it slows.

"Mom says we should post no-loitering signs and hire a security guy for the house. Full-time." Ty's voice is carefully pitched. Newscaster voice.

Flesh presses against the windows as the limo eases forward. The driver honks the horn.

"Probably a good idea," I say. "Considering."

Behind the house, Ty gets out of the car. He comes to get my door, and I move as fast as I can up the steps and through the door.

Ty still won't look at me, a mask of neutrality on his

face. The roses feel ridiculous in my arms. Heavy, like an accusation.

"Ty," I start, "I'm sorry—I haven't been very—" A parade of words fills the blank I can't say.

Loving.

Present.

Attentive.

Good.

Careful with you.

Ty's shoulders droop, but he smiles at me. It's not a wide-open sky.

"Come on." He leads the way down the hall, to the TV room.

"I feel like an idiot now."

He opens the door.

There's another bunch of flowers on the coffee table. Silver, red, and white balloons on metallic ribbons float above the vase. One of them says *Happy Anniversary!*

A satin-edged red blanket is spread picnic-style on the carpet. A redneck wedding reception is laid out on it.

Anniversary?

He's been so calm, so easygoing. So available to me in spite of everything. So wise with his grief, with how he expresses it. So consistent, so mature. I forgot how old he is.

Or rather, how young. Am I the first girl he's kissed?

"Our anniversary," I say. "Um. One month, right?"

It runs though me like actual pain. In the center of my chest is a mass of nerves, a ball of razored twine, my heart a red, raw mass of blood and feeling.

My first flowers were a bouquet of wild daisies Joshua gave me in ninth grade. And a card with a poem he'd written inside. The basis for his first hit.

"Ty," I start to say, turning around to face him.

He startles me, surging forward, stopping whatever I would say with his lips. Grabbing on to me like he means it.

"Ty," I try, between kissing and breathing.

"Stop," he says. "You don't have to say it, Roxy."

I bite the words back.

Ty nods. His eyes are shielded, and so is the half smile he gives me. "We can go back to not talking about it."

"Okay," I whisper. But it's not. I see that.

The world is spinning fast.

19

THE HOLE IN THE NET

We pretend to go back to the way we were. Time goes by, and I don't mark it. Neither does Ty. He finishes the album. I keep searching Birdie sites.

Grandma starts grumbling about me getting a job. About me going out. Getting a GED. Maybe going to community college. About how I need to have a plan for life.

Ty gets busier. Artie flies him out to LA, to meet people, to record more songs—out there this time. Livie goes with him, for now. Although I wonder how long it will be before she signs guardianship over to Artie or if Ty will emancipate himself just like his brother did. Livie will want control over the money for as long as possible. She's learned how to hover.

Ty assures us he knows what he's doing. Says it's what

he wants. The album, the fame, the everything-that-comes-next.

Even though he still calls, even though we still get together when he's around, it's different.

I can already feel the distance between us, from the one-month anniversary. Even though he tried to take it back. It showed us that it was untenable, what we had.

Then one day he's leaving to go to LA to stay. No more back-and-forth; he has to focus on finishing the album and promotion. Livie's going with him. He didn't ask me to come.

I don't know what I would have said if he had.

He comes to say good-bye on his dirt bike. In my grandma's yard, he says he'll see me soon. He'll call all the time. And any time I want to come out, he will be so happy to see me.

I know it's over by the closed way he looks at me. Despite his words. He wants more than I can offer.

"It's going to be okay, Rox," he says.

I want to scream that he's found a way out of the pain too soon. That this isn't real, isn't the way to do it. But life goes on, the world goes on.

"I love you," he says. "However it needs to be. I love you. I have since we were kids, you know."

I wonder at Ty's heart, at how he doesn't close himself off from me, even now. How he's so capable, so ready to love.

If I'll ever experience those feelings again. Or if I want to.

Lillian Leitzel knew what she wanted. Always. She got it: a private dressing room, a red carpet rolled into the center ring. If it was muddy, an attendant would carry her all the way to her rope.

She demanded a private railcar with a piano. As the Queen of the Circus she insisted she be assigned a personal maid.

She was a tiny, muscular tornado. Four foot nine and weighed ninety-five pounds. She had incredibly small feet, which added to her fairylike impression as she moved through the air.

I can imagine her, a real person, here now. Watching me with her hands on her hips.

She would know what to do. What she wanted. She wouldn't be trapped in an empty expanse.

I imagine her walking into the center ring, blowing kisses. A roustabout would hold out the rope.

"Did you get it right this time?" she'd ask from behind the smile for the crowd.

The roustabout kneeled to let her stand upon his leg. "Yes, Miss Leitzel."

She hit him the last time he got her rigging wrong. She had stormed into the men's tent, screaming and hitting. Shoving men twice her size aside until she reached him.

And then she'd later apologized to the others. Handed out twenties like they were penny candies.

Lillian Leitzel knew who she was. She knew what she could do.

She would never be trapped, suspended in space. Like I am now.

After Ty leaves for LA, I sink into an endless series of days filled with empty routine. I add a few Ty-centric Birdies to my Tumblr to see him how they see him.

Ty sends me an advance link to the first single. It's good, but not great. He probably knows that, but it doesn't matter. It'll go platinum, easy.

And it does. The critics say it's a good "first effort"—damning the whole thing with faint praise, but being gentle. It's obvious to everyone that he's not his brother.

Grandma and I stay up late to watch one of Ty's TV appearances. It's hard to believe it's him, even though I've already seen the transformation that Artie can wring from a skinny kid.

He looks more cool, more sophisticated than he ever was. Heavy work boots and tight black jeans. New haircut, shaved sides, long in front.

It makes me tense, watching him perform. Seeing him like that.

I don't realize I'm sitting up, fists on my knees, letting

out tense sighs until the song is over and Grandma laughs at me.

"There, safe, on the other side," she says, muting the commercial that follows the audience applause. "He made it after all."

"Made it?" I can't keep the edge of venom out of my voice. "He just got out there. It's all just begun for him."

Grandma shakes her head as she levers herself out of the recliner. "Ty saw it all. He'll be more prepared than Joshua."

Her eyes mist up anytime she says his name. "Joshua, bless him. He was so feeling. All heart, that child." She dabs at her eyes with the Kleenex she keeps tucked in her sleeve. "Bless Joshua," she sighs, tucking the tissue back.

Grandma grabs the handle of her oxygen tank and pulls it behind her as she shuffles toward the hall.

"Nearly forgot. Something came for you," Grandma calls from the hallway. "I put it on your bed."

I turn off the TV and the lights, lock the doors, and walk back to my room.

A large white envelope sits on my bed. The return address is the seal for Bayard University, a private school outside Atlanta.

Air huffs though my nose.

"Subtle, Grandma," I mutter. But I flip it over and tear it open anyway.

It doesn't make sense. I stare at the letter, on official letterhead, trying to figure it out.

My eyes fall to the first line.

I am writing to inform you that you have been granted provisional admission to the College of Liberal Arts at Bayard University.

When I saw the envelope, I thought my grandma had written away for it. A typical, general information packet, probably with application materials.

My eyes flick over the letter. Phrases jump out: *upon successful completion* and *summer and fall enrollment.*

It doesn't make any sense. My grades were always okay, good but not good enough for me to be wooed for some kind of early acceptance program. What's more, I haven't exactly been doing my online coursework since coming back to Georgia.

And I haven't applied for any admission to any college anywhere. Provisional or early or regular or any of it.

Then I see the thing that changes everything else, that shakes my brain loose. On the page where it breaks down the fees owed in the future—tuition, room and board for the dorms and meal plan—on the line labeled *Amount Due,* it reads *Paid in Full.*

Every. Single. Item.

Anger surges through me. *Ty.* It had to be him.

If I want to go to college, I'll do it *myself.*

I pull out my cell and call Ty.

"Rox?" His voice is muffled. In the background I hear voices of others. He's probably at an after-party, celebrating his performance on *The Late Late Show*.

"I don't need your charity." My voice is shaking. The sudden flood of so much emotion after the prolonged numbness makes me feel stronger than I have since Joshua died.

"What?"

"I don't know if I even *want* to go to college, so your *paying for it* is making me hate the idea!"

I'm furious. It's none of his business if I swim or if I drown in my sorrow.

Some things you never get over. Never.

"I don't know what you're talking about." Ty's voice is open. Sincere in a way that LA hasn't trained out of him yet.

"You didn't apply to Bayard for me? Didn't pay the entire tuition?"

"What? No, Rox. Not that I wouldn't—you can always call me for help—"

"I'll stand or fall on my own, jerkface."

"I know that," Ty says. His voice is trying to soothe an enraged bull. "I know. Hell, you've always been like that. I don't even know what you're talking about."

And he doesn't. That openness. I would know if he were lying.

Artie? Did Artie do this? To make sure I stay out of the picture?

I hang up on Ty. Call Artie before he can tell her I'm raging.

Even though she's probably right there with him.

She screens her calls, so she doesn't pick up. I don't leave a message, instead hanging up and calling the number again.

I hang up and call for an hour straight. Then I get an idea. I go out to Grandma's chair and get her cell phone and dial Artie's number. When the answering message comes on, I play Ty's version of "Orpheus's Last Lyric." While that records, I call on my phone, tying up her line completely.

I alternate with the two phones until I no longer get the voicemail cue please-leave-a-message. I've filled it up.

Then I keep calling.

"Damn it, Roxanne," Artie answers, finally.

"Did you pay my tuition to Bayard University?"

"What? No." She sounds sincere, but it's Artie. She learned to fake sincerity in the crib. "What the hell is going on?"

"Someone applied for me and paid my entire way."

"Bully for you."

"It wasn't you?"

"No."

A silent *I dare you to talk* empty line hiss.

I break it. "Was there an addendum to his will? Is that what this is?"

"No. It's all settled. Nothing more."

It doesn't make sense. It had to be one of them. There is no other answer. I didn't apply, and even with my trust money from Joshua, I don't have this kind of cash lying around. Most of it's invested, and if I want to get it I can, but I have to jump through several hoops first.

"Is that all, Roxanne?" Artie's voice is clipped.

I sigh. "Sure. Thanks, Artie. I guess."

Artie sighs too. "We're all doing the best we can, Roxanne. Maybe try cutting yourself a break. Maybe just take it as a gift. Something you deserve. Have you asked your grandmother? Maybe she found the money somewhere."

It doesn't seem possible, but nothing else could make sense at this point.

I hang up and take the letter to my grandma.

"Did you do this?" I hand her the letter.

"Oh, sugar, congratulations!" Her face is transformed by a smile.

"Where did the money come from? Did you mortgage the house? You didn't have to—"

"What? No!" Grandma smiles down at the letter. "They gave you a scholarship, I bet!"

Something my grades would never allow, but I don't

argue. Instead I kiss her good night, leave her in bed reading mystery novels.

Back on my bed, I pull the covers up around my shoulders, curled on the mattress like a sea snail, feeling soft and vulnerable, a thin shell of blanket no real protection at all.

On my desk next to the laptop, the envelope from Bayard University gleams expensive eggshell white. The color of rich, protected dreams.

I can't think of what to do. I can't imagine who would do such a thing for me.

There is only one person apart from Grandma who has loved me that much.

Thinking about Joshua and the loss of how he felt about me, how he saw me, is like riding a hateful roller coaster in the dark. The sudden plunge you don't see but still expect, a wrenching side to side as you race into the grief and the guilt.

Joshua's eyes when I got doxed—was that when he thought I'd be better off without him? He'd always seen me as strong, as someone who could protect herself, set her elbows out, plant her feet wide and stand against them.

When did that change?

When did *everything* change? Even Joshua? What did I miss?

I want to scream at everyone. I want to scream the

questions we should have asked, scream urgency that we pursue the answers. Was he okay? Why did he buy all that real estate to hand out like party favors? Why did he give up writing the kind of music he actually *liked*? Why did he give every bit of himself away?

Why did we let him?

Is that what this college thing is all about? Just one more gift he arranged for when the time was right? When does it all end?

At the time we couldn't do anything else but accept what Joshua told us. It was his ride, but he wasn't the one driving. First there was the album, the debut one, then the tour. Then a new album and rehearsing for a new tour. In between the two, he turned seventeen.

He was emancipated. He set up accounts for his mother and Ty. He bought houses and all those many other, glittering things.

We thought he was enjoying the hard-won fruits of his success. We thought he was looking to the future. Did he even want a future?

He wasn't strong enough for this. And it would never have been over, even if he'd stopped recording and touring. It was too late to go back, too late to become anonymous, too late to say that what you really wanted was something else.

Not this. Not this life, this fame. This "dream" that anyone would kill for.

It wore on him, caused a small rip to tear completely apart, pulling him into separate pieces.

Those houses he bought for everyone—they were bits of permanence, refuges from and for the people closest to him. With the exception of the LA mansion, the houses were away from the spotlight. Actual homes. Walls to protect us.

When he was the one who needed protection.

What did we do instead? Paraded him around like a circus act, microphone to microphone, spotlight to spotlight. We took away his music and replaced it—replaced *him*—with *Joshua Blackbird*.

And I told him the story of an aerialist who would fall, but who first dared the world to watch as she dislocated her shoulder again and again, pretending to be something that could fly.

At what point did he realize that he hated what he'd become?

At what point did I merely join the line of people forcing the transformation rather than someone fighting to help him?

It makes nausea churn in my stomach, a self-loathing sludge. I roll over and pick up my phone. I touch the screen, then close my eyes against my room. Against the sight of the envelope and everything else.

And listen to Joshua's voice, trapped forever in voice

mail. We'd argued, and I was angry and didn't go to a rehearsal with him. I don't even know *why* I was so mad at him.

He'd called me. I had sent the call straight to voice mail.

"Hey, Rox, I'm sorry." His voice is tired and a little shy, murmured like he's holding his phone too close to his mouth, or like he's trying to be quiet. "Answer the phone or call me, okay? I love you. Everything'll be okay, I promise."

"Liar," I breathe. And for a moment, it's like talking to him.

I hit Repeat.

I lie in my bed and listen to his voice, listen to his voice talking just to me, and for the first time, I'm able to hear him without tears, and it's like being held. Like a warm secret curling into my ear.

I stop playing Joshua's voice and don't let myself think about how long I've avoided Speed's calls and texts. I just scroll down till I find his number. Because I need to talk to a friend. We both loved Joshua, and therefore loved each other, at least a little.

"Roxy!" Speed's voice is filled with California sunshine. In the background, I can hear sounds of a party.

"Hey, Speed, sorry I haven't been . . . in touch." The words are paltry, but not so much that I shouldn't say them.

"It's okay. I missed you, but I get it." Speed, always shoring up my weakness, his voice like his presence back then, and even now over the phone, palpable and lifting me up. Like he's draped my arm over his shoulders and is helping me walk.

I can picture him sitting with a leg bouncing or pacing in the room, moving or shaking or tapping, energy thrumming through him, a constant hum.

He carries the phone into a quiet room. We talk for a little while, just catching up. He asks about my grandma; I ask about his parents. We talk about the tribute album, and I compliment his cover, which was so much more fitting than Angel's. Which brings us to Ty and his version of "Orpheus's Last Lyric," and where they both are now.

"What's it like?" I ask. "Playing for Ty?"

Speed lets out a deep sigh, like he knew I would ask the question, and like it's something he's thought about endlessly already.

"It's good," he says. "But it's not the same."

A world of possibilities and missed possibilities in that phrase. *Not the same.*

"Because he's not Joshua," I say.

"He's smart, and he's okay as a musician," Speed says. "I mean he's plenty good. He's not Joshua—we all know that. Hell, *he* knows that. It's just . . . weird, you know? Like we're all just trying to replace the person who brought us here."

I can't keep it to myself anymore, the real reason I called.

The envelope waits for me, beside my laptop.

I tell him about the university acceptance and the paid tuition.

"That's great, Roxy," he says. "Are you gonna go?"

So very Speed, to ignore the glaring question to ask a different one.

"I don't know," I say. "I just really need to know where the money's coming from. Who did this? Who applied for me?"

"I wish it was me, sweet girl, but I don't got that kind of money."

"I know. Who does? It's not Ty, it's not Artie, and it's not my grandma."

"Maybe it's a label exec or something?"

No. No way. They throw money at a problem, sure, but they certainly don't sit down and fill out an application and write an essay.

Besides, I'm not even there. In LA. Where anyone would even think of me, much less be moved to do something like this.

I can tell from Speed's voice that he's humoring me,

because—typical, wonderful Speed—he doesn't really care where the money comes from. He's got some *the universe says* mythos he goes for, even if he usually keeps it to himself. Probably thinks *the universe* arranged this as a karmic debt to me after what happened.

I drop the subject and make a few more vague promises about visiting. Then the rest of the conversation winds down.

"I should go," I say.

"Thanks for calling, Roxy."

I smile. "Thanks for picking up, and for forgiving me when I didn't."

"I'm always here for you."

"Thanks. I . . ." I can't say any more. Like this perverse need for absolute honesty won't let a fake promise past my lips. The same thing that won't let me tell Ty I love him, because it's not the kind of love that he's hoping for.

"It's okay," Speed says. "I'll talk to you soon."

I take a deep breath. "Take care of him, okay?"

Take care of Ty. When neither of us could take care of his brother.

Speed's voice is soothing. "Hey. Yeah. But he's going to be okay. When you come here, you'll see that."

"Yeah, when I come there." Unspoken: *not happening soon*. Speed hears that last part.

"Love you, Rox. Be kind to yourself . . . okay?"

My eyes sting with held-back tears. "Love you too."

I end the call.

I move to my computer, wake it up, and go online, searching the university's name.

I click through splash pages and promotional materials and see that the application process is entirely online. Which means I should be able to see what got sent in for me.

It would be proof that someone did go through this whole process for me, even if it feels beyond surreal right now.

I click the application link. I see a "log in" option and a "create an account" option.

To log in, I need an email and a password.

I enter my email.

Nothing.

The cursor blinks at me.

I blink back.

In the morning I can call and claim my email got hacked or something, and I'm locked out, and can they let me set up a new account so I can access my new student profile?

But that would require waiting until morning. Would mean sitting here staring at the thing, wondering who did it. What it all means.

Impatience burns through me like anger, a fire that makes my teeth hurt.

I make myself unclench my jaw.

There's a *forgot your username?* link and a *forgot your password?* link.

If I use one, can I use the other? Are there security protocols in place like that?

I sit, chewing my ragged nails when it hits me.

I have another email account.

Hastily I enter rox01@theblackbirdfound.org.

We all got emails and foundation memberships when Ty set it up.

The login accepts.

"Bingo," I breathe.

Now a password.

I have no clue. I type my usual password— *WonderWoman**—and get nothing.

I'm about to hit the "forgot my password" button when it hits me.

The password has to be a combination of numbers, capital and lowercase letters, and must include at least one symbol.

I type *LillianLeitzel<3*.

It works.

My heart thunders in my chest. My racing pulse rattles my fingers, hovering over the keyboard.

The person who did this *knows me*. Really knows me. Knows I'd want to stay near my grandma. Knows LA isn't for me.

They knew about my Blackbird Foundation email account. They knew about my love for Lillian Leitzel.

There's only one person alive with all those pieces.

Ty lied to me. It *had* to be him.

But why? There would be no reason to lie once I called him out on it, would there?

I study the links on my new student profile. I can upload a picture, can write a blurb "about me," can indicate interest in certain university clubs or activities.

There is a university bursar's office. I click on it and go to my account, where I definitively see that I did not get a scholarship. Or a loan. Or any special waiver of tuition.

Paid in Full.

I click back out and find the application itself, with a pane that says "view." I click it.

Bayard University has a renowned history department.

I wonder if Ty listed history as my potential major. I scroll down to the bottom of the application, see a short essay portion.

Ty knows his way around a melody, but I doubt essay writing is his thing. At any rate, I have to see what he said.

If you could have dinner with any person, living or dead, who would it be and why?

A painful laugh cuts my windpipe. Because the answer is so simple, so obvious, but I'd bet money that Ty over-thought it. Probably picked Leitzel, while the answer is his brother.

I wouldn't care about the dinner part. Just one more conversation. One more moment to see him, to touch him. One chance to find out what I could have done. *Should* have done.

20

THE HUNGER SONG OF
THE LAZARUS BIRD

My eyes sting. As a voice echoes in my head and memory as I read the short essay.

If you could have dinner with any person, living or dead, who would it be and why?

I'd meet myself—the me I'm going to be. The one who will be okay. The one who's more certain. I'd like to be in a place where I can let myself accept unconditionally—let me be a monument to something fleeting that has passed. And then let me build something new.

I know that it's impossible to hold back change or to think that we're ever done changing. The moment we cease changing is the moment we stop growing. Still we hold tight to our injuries, to blame, and let them bind us, the ropes so tight that we lose feeling.

We need to forgive life, forgive change, and forgive ourselves for becoming something else.

So the place I'd like to get to is that of acceptance, forgiveness for it all. That's the me I'd like to meet, the one who accepts my mistakes, how everything went wrong, but who's okay with letting go . . . someone who's not drowning, but waving.

The voice in my head. The voice reading these words to me. I pull it into my heart like a blanket.

I reread it, this *brief essay* that says so much. That references the poem Ms. Kearney taught us, the Stevie Smith poem. That hopes for acceptance. For forgiveness.

For everything to be okay.

I feel it before I can consciously think it. The feeling is like a trembling, feathered creature, sitting in my chest. Charged with life. Waiting to take to the air.

Joshua.

Joshua wrote this.

When? How?

Am I really thinking this? Am I really thinking that he's *alive?*

It crashes into me. The memorial without a casket. The unbidden mental image of the devastation of a drowned body. One we never could find. Unrecognizable, devoured. Gone, as if it never existed.

The thousands of television commentators, speculating ghoulishly about the remains.

We never found his body.

What if he's alive?

I hear a small, high laugh. It sounds unhinged. It sounds on the verge of a breakdown. I force myself to take deep breaths and let them out slowly.

I reread the essay.

It's absolutely Joshua.

It wants so much. Such giant, beautiful, desires for a lifetime. A small, simple, everything word: *acceptance.*

It echoes "Orpheus's Last Lyric."

Without thinking, with the high whine of giddy laughter echoing in my head, I print the application and then go online to the BlueBirdie sites. I dig and unfilter and unblock the hashtags, and eventually I find the subset—the death deniers.

The crazies.

I'm one of them now.

JOSHUA BLACKBIRD IS ALIVE! a banner reads.

At first, it's layers of old photos and tired hope. Flat denial and no substance underneath. Or very little substance. A user named BlackAndBlueBird deconstructs the myth of Orpheus—how Orpheus returned from the underworld after losing his love forever. How Orpheus wandered in the wilds, grieving, until he was attacked and killed, torn apart by the maenads, wild women. Some versions even imply that Orpheus sought the death.

The parallels are obvious, and BlackAndBlueBird isn't the first person to make them. Orpheus is Joshua, the lost love is Angel (they insert pictures from their last meeting), the wild women are the hungry fans, specifically Mira.

They post her picture and the leaked photos of Joshua's stab wound. The ambulance and long-lens shots of him going into court.

But where the myth required Orpheus to die, BlackAndBlueBird says for Joshua it meant giving up his music. That the "death" was symbolic, a death of the way of life he had before that moment.

A huff of disgust presses out of my mouth. Feels half-baked. I keep looking.

A few clicks later, I find JOSHUA BLACKBIRD FAKED HIS DEATH. Roundly ridiculed by commenter after commenter, the post by NotYourDog has photos, and it's these that grab my attention.

The text talks about the boat accident. About the fact that even though no other craft were recorded in the deep water off the island, that doesn't mean no one else was there. It includes links to the next closest harbors, beaches, boat launches. Includes nautical miles to buoys, piers, land, and island.

What? They think Joshua could swim that far? Or that someone could meet him with a boat? Who? We were all there on the boat, already with him.

And even if Joshua did hire someone to help him, there's no way they would keep that secret. Not with so much money to be made from the exposé.

Of course, NotYourDog doesn't explain away any of these questions. Just throws the possibility of how Joshua might have done it out there like so many cluster bombs— how it could have happened, if you don't look at it too closely or think about it too long. The theory like fairy-tale magic, with no evidence underneath.

What NotYourDog does instead is insert pictures from Joshua's memorial service, spinning from one big question to another. The photos are sun drenched, all the more jarringly wrong, the perfection of that day.

The remembered pain of then and the actual pain of now collide in my chest. It's like looking through a magic mirror at a place that I barely remember. That caused so much heart-erupting destruction.

I don't remember standing there talking. I don't remember sitting there listening. It's like it happened to someone else.

But there I am in the picture, in the garden of stone monuments. A telephoto lens capturing my shock-numbed face. On one side of me sits Ty with Livie next to him. On the other side of me is Speed. Next to him, the rest of the band.

A second picture captures a different angle—must have been a different paparazzo. Someone standing at the gates, or perched along the wall, taking pictures to sell as we bled.

In the second photo you can see Artie and the label execs. Joshua's legal team, second-string agents, the tour dancers, video directors, stage managers, roadies, security guys, costume designers, pyrotechnic employees, the whole cavalcade from the tour, from his career beyond it.

Behind them, in a mass of people, I spot Rick and Dan.

Who isn't here? the caption reads.

No one. No one is missing. Just asking the question doesn't make it so. There's nothing else. It's clickbait, a teaser post—meant to make a Birdie subscribe to the feed. Follow NotYourDog.

I scroll through the more recent posts. There's another shot from the funeral with a screaming caption.

WHO IS IN THE SHADOWS?

I scan the funeral picture. This one is from a higher angle, like the photographer climbed a ladder or a tree to get a better shot of the crowd of mourners.

But the resolution of the shot isn't as high. Almost as if it was an amateur camera or camera phone.

A Birdie in a tree.

I laugh, and it's the unhinged one again.

I close my eyes and force slow breaths through my nose. Pick up the printed college application and reread the essay.

It's him. Joshua wrote this.

I have to keep digging.

I lean toward the computer screen and study the high-angle picture. What figure in the shadows?

Who isn't here?

Who's in the shadows?

I have to laugh at the drama. At the questions without answers.

There's no one in the shadows. I've searched the shaded periphery twice. It's a question without an answer, without substance, without—

I see two blurry lines in the shade beside a mausoleum on the edge of the shot. It could almost be legs? Two legs, propped out, like someone is standing there, on the edge of everything, leaning against the mausoleum.

Hiding. Leaning around the small stone building to see and not be seen.

My eyes burn from staring.

I blink and rub them and look again.

It's definitely there. Two long shadows, a pair of legs. I see it now.

Unless it's something else.

I rush back in my grief-hazed memory. Try to remember that particular mausoleum. Did it have anything on that side that could cast that shape? That could look like . . .

I scroll up through more posts. Then it's blown up, the same picture I've been looking at, or think I have.

WHO ISN'T HERE? The headline blares again.

The picture is not of the mausoleum, but of a shaded weeping willow on the opposite, farther side of the shot.

Someone stands underneath the hanging branches. You can vaguely see a dark black coat, and two black-clad legs, planted far apart.

This is it? This is the proof?

It could be anyone. It could be a groundskeeper. Or someone who wandered away from the press of people.

NotYourDog's caption reads The HOLLYWOOD FOR-EVER CEMETERY.

The text goes on to give all the theoretical reasons why the figure means something. How it's important that the person was partially obscured behind the hanging branches of the tree. How the long coat and black pants, as well as the position of the feet, indicate that this person was attending the funeral, watching it, albeit from a distance and from the shadows.

Someone was watching the service like it was a matinee. What *was* the performance? *Being Joshua Blackbird,* that was the theater. The only way out was to give one final show. Cue the curtain. But to pull that off? There had to be *someone*, one person Joshua trusted with his life. Or in this case, his death.

I click back to the original *WHO'S IN THE SHADOWS?* post.

Underneath it is the usual flotsam and jetsam of Internet commenters. Fellow Birdies crying or congratulating NotYourDog. Trolls ridiculing the whole idea, but more than that, ridiculing the legions of Birdie fans. And there're few hopeful fellow believers, making a feast of crumbs.

I can no longer avoid the underlying pain, beneath the bounding hope that Joshua *is* alive. And while I am still holding that against-all-odds hope in my chest like a spark of sacred flame—

It can't be true. Could it? How could he do something like that?

In my mind the black-and-white security camera footage plays: Joshua on the deck of the boat. The smile that changed into sorrow.

Saying good-bye.

Did he do that to me? Did he want me to believe he was dead?

It whiplashes through me, a high-tension wire snapped and slicing. The pain is too much, like another death, holding both possibilities in my mind.

A hope that hurts as much as acceptance of loss.

My hand shakes as I pick up the printed application and reread the essay.

This time I see it as something else. Not just a message *from* him, but a message *for me*. He knew I'd read this.

It's like a dare.

21

HOLLYWOOD FOREVER CEMETERY

t won't take me long to pack. It won't take long to explain to Grandma that I want to visit my friends in LA. This actually makes her happy.

The more I think about it, the more I think that someone has to be keeping something from me. They have to know. Either they know who paid my tuition or they know that Joshua is alive.

Just thinking it makes me feel like my brain is spinning, twisting, on a trapeze.

Someone knows what's going on.

Even though I've talked to Ty, and Artie, and Speed. Even though they've all denied it. It's not the same when you're not standing in front of someone.

Over the phone, it's easier to lie. They need to see my face.

And I need to do something, need to try to find him. If he's alive, he's waiting for me.

He sent me the application like a message. Like a hidden Easter egg or scavenger hunt.

I think of Ty.

I remember holding him as we cried after the memorial service. Or was it only me crying? When I thought we were both falling apart, was it just one-sided and I was too blinded by tears to see?

He was always so certain that Joshua hadn't committed suicide. Was it because he really knew that Joshua was alive?

How Joshua intended his death to look? Like an accident?

My certainty and anger twist. This wasn't some criminal mastermind waiting to deceive us all. It was the boy next door, the boy I loved, always loved, struggling to keep himself together. He either thought we all would be better without him or that he'd be better off without us. Maybe I am the bridge connecting the two, preventing either from being a certainty?

Someone has to know.

I have to see Ty.

I have to see him. Have to look into his eyes when I ask.

Does Artie know as well? In her rush to capitalize on Joshua's death—what she called "cementing his legacy"—was she instead just making a last, desperate cash grab before the crap hit the fans?

Because how would everyone respond if they learned he *faked it?*

No secret keeps forever.

The Birdies won't respond with love, no matter what they think now. No matter *I'd give anything to have him back!* protestations. They'd respond with rage and shunning. Cutting him up for the affront, for using them. Not even Artie could spin such a story. The media and the bloggers would overwhelm her with a virtuous rage, even as they milked the story themselves. Artie's career would be ruined.

I don't hate the idea.

I throw in clothes and makeup, toothbrush, power cords, notebooks.

A derisive voice narrates my every move.

You realize this is insane. You realize you're cracking up. You'll end up at Haven View with Mira. Joshua's alive? Listen to yourself! This is a delusion. What will you do when you see the truth? What will you do when it is in your face?

When you finally accept that he chose death over life with you?

I acknowledge the voice. I might be chasing a dream. Or a dangerous delusion.

But *someone* filled out this application. *Someone* paid my tuition.

The zipper growls low as I close the duffel bag. I pull

on cropped fatigues and desert combat boots, loop canvas
BDU belts over my hips, and tug on a tank top and ripped
T-shirt.

I glance in the mirror and regret it.

My eyes are wide and staring, sparking with fanaticism
and the pressure of napalm hope.

In the reflection I see the printed application sitting
on the bed. I turn and pick it up.

The page is my talisman, my magical object. I have a
quest. I have a purpose.

And a dare.

A few hours later, a cab comes to take me to the airport. I
kiss Grandma and promise to call when I get there.

On the plane I sleep. We land in LA in the afternoon.
I get in line for a cab.

Ty doesn't know I'm coming. I don't text or call. I
don't care if it feels cloak-and-dagger. What I'm thinking
is cloak-and-dagger.

If they commit me, maybe I need it.

Or maybe I'm right.

While I wait, I call Grandma and tell her I'm here safe.
Remind her to lock the doors after she airs out the house.

She tells me she loves me, tells me to "have fun
out there."

It feels so on point it hurts. "Out there"—like I may as well be on the moon.

My brain is tired of holding possibilities and meanings. Tired of holding a possibility that hurts as much as the previous certainty, that hurts just to imagine the absence of. Tired of guilt, sidestepping grief for this desperation. A conspiracy of hopes.

I get in the cab and give the driver the address of what used to be Joshua's, and is now Ty's, ocean-side mansion.

I sit back, watching the afternoon sun light the city—it's ready for its close-up now—as we drive away from LAX, past industrial tourism developments, convention halls, liquor stores, and gas stations, into the satellite-to-wealthier neighborhoods, then to the edges of wealthy ones. Then come the wealthy neighborhoods. Giant palm trees and ornate gates, security cameras and massive houses.

Then suddenly we're there. The cab pulls up to the wrought-iron gates at the top of the driveway.

There's a speaker on the driver's side.

"Press the button," I tell the driver. I put down my window so I can speak to whoever answers.

"Yes?"

"It's Roxy. Roxanne Stewart. I'm Ty's friend," I say. "I'm here to visit."

"One moment."

A pause, presumably while the approved visitors list or superiors are consulted.

The gate swings open, and the voice comes back though the speaker. "Park in front, please."

At the front of the house, I pay the driver and get out my suitcase. The taxi follows the swooping curve of the driveway back around and out.

I carry my suitcase up the steps. The door opens before I can knock. An unfamiliar security guard stands there, chewing on a toothpick and squinting at me.

"Is Ty here?" I ask inanely.

"No, he's not." The guard doesn't move out of the way or invite me in.

"When will he come back?"

"I can't say."

I shift the suitcase to my other hand. "Well, he invited me to come."

"I haven't received instructions."

He sounds like a careful robot, attempting to handle a bomb.

"Listen, is Artie around? Do you have her number? Call or text and then get out of my way, please."

The meat-robot's eyes go flat. "Wait here."

The door closes in my face. I get out my phone and text Ty. Surprise, I'm here! Can't get into the house—will you take care of it? Where are you?

I hit Send. Look at the clipped message after it goes through. Send a puking smiley face to soften it up and to remind him of back home.

The door opens.

"I am instructed to hold your bag here. Ms. Malfa says she will send a car to take you to the restaurant where they will be having dinner."

"Okay. Thanks." I hand over my suitcase.

It feels ridiculous, waiting on the front step like a door-to-door salesman, but I don't want to go inside without Ty. It feels too much like a time warp, and I know looking around that room will remind me too much of the night Joshua died.

My phone dings.

Wow, great! Artie says she sent a car. Can't wait to see you! After Ty's message is a GIF of a happy cat flailing and falling off a treadmill.

It makes me smile, in spite of my anxiety about accusing him. In spite of my anxiety about what I will learn, or have to face.

A black luxury sedan eventually pulls up to the gate. It drives up to where I'm waiting, and a driver gets out.

"Ms. Stewart?" she says, as she walks around the front of the car to open my door.

"Hi, yes," I say.

"I'm Sasha." The driver flashes an incandescent smile at me. Her teeth are perfect. Her pale skin is perfect, poreless; her green eyes are ringed by gorgeous, thick, curled lashes. Her lips are lush to the point of looking unreal. Her beauty is shocking.

"Sorry," I stammer, realizing I'm staring. "I forgot how beautiful people are out here."

"Thanks," she says. "You fit right in."

It's a lie, but I can't help the stupid, momentary glow it gives me.

She closes the door and walks back to her side and gets behind the wheel. We coast down the driveway and out the gate.

"I'm to take you to Mephisto's. Mr. Blackbird and his party will meet you there. They're finishing a recording session. I'm afraid you'll be a little early for dinner, but you're to feel free to order appetizers and a beverage while you wait. The charges will go to Ms. Malfa's account."

"They're at Aepolis Studios? I thought the album was done," I say, more to make conversation than any real interest.

"I wouldn't know about that," she says flatly. Then, as though to make up for her loyalty to the person who pays her salary, offers a smile in the rearview mirror.

I return the smile and offer an understanding "Of course."

I lean back against the plush leather seat. A small vase attached to the armrest holds a single white rose. A chilled water bottle and cocktail napkins sit in the cup holder nearest me.

Outside my window, gate after gate goes by. A few dogs are walked, by professional dog walkers, probably. Landscape crews go to work perfecting perfection.

Security gates, security boxes, security cameras.

Thinking of the Birdie blogs, I suddenly have a much better idea than sitting at an empty table waiting for Ty to arrive.

The Hollywood Forever Cemetery can't be that far away. It's prime real estate as much as any of this. Houses of the dead are just as valuable as houses of the living.

I should go look at the mausoleum where the blurred shadow was. And see the layout of the area, the weeping willow, just check it out. Maybe I'll find something there.

Joshua's memorial, for example. With its completed plaque.

It wasn't there at the funeral. The etched portion was delivered later. Artie sent me a photo of it. But I haven't actually seen it.

What if it can tell me something?

"Actually," I say, "could we take a detour?"

"You want to see the Hollywood sign?" Sasha asks, smiling. Indulging a tourist.

"No. I mean, yes, but I'd like to go to the cemetery first, please. The Hollywood Forever Cemetery?"

There's a time-stutter moment of silence, and immediately I know that Sasha won't take me.

"Well, sweetie, people will be waiting for you—they might have wrapped up early?"

"Yeah, I don't think so," I said. "Please, I just want to visit his memorial site. I was his girlfriend. His real-life one."

"I'm supposed to take you to Mephisto's," Sasha says, no longer meeting my eyes in the rearview.

"I'm sure Ty's good for any extra mileage." I can feel the edge in my voice, a driving bass line of insistence.

"I'm sorry," she says. "I was asked to take you to the restaurant. And I need this job."

"Fine. Pull over, please." I push up the lock and crack open the door.

Sasha curses.

The door alarm chimes like a demented elevator. The road swoops by below my feet. I push the door farther open.

Sasha pulls to the curb. Blaring horns sound as cars swoop around us.

My safety belt is off before we come to a stop. I'm out the door before Sasha can put it in park.

"Wait! What do I tell them?"

"Tell them that you wouldn't take me where I asked to go, and so I got out."

"Wait! Okay! I'll take you, just let me call—"

"No."

"Just—" Sasha looks at me like I've grown a hand from the top of my head and that hand is giving her the finger.

Like she thinks I'm crazy, and dangerous.

"I really don't want to lose my job," she says, gesturing at me in an *easy, there* move. "How about this: I drive you, and I don't call in until we've left the cemetery. I'll give you at least ten minutes in there. Cool?"

I consider for a moment, because I'm not even sure why I suddenly need to go and why I want to go alone.

"Sure," I say. "Sure let's do that."

I'd be slower walking, and she'd call it in, anyway, to save her job.

I get back in the car. Sasha pulls out and U-turns against traffic. It's a short drive, a few turns, past storefronts and down wide-canyon roads before she turns down an unlikely-looking side street.

"Here we are," she says, unnecessarily.

The gates are open. A few tourists stroll over the lushly manicured lawn, brochures or phones out to find their favorite dead celebrities.

The final resting place of the stars.

When stars flame out, they fall.

We drive slowly on narrow roads, past monuments, around mourners and tourists.

"That's got Valentino in there. You know him? A bunch of kids today don't." Sasha gestures ahead of us to a large, churchlike mausoleum across the road from a moat. "The original heartthrob."

My head is split in half with the small talk, my heart accelerating as we draw closer to Joshua's memorial.

A stone with no body beneath it. Just one more empty home Joshua paid for.

What a strange thought.

Sasha waits while a young couple cross the road. One of the girls peers directly at us, trying to see who sits behind the dark windows.

Sasha drives slowly forward, pulling around the moat. "There was bedlam when Valentino died. A bona fide riot in New York. Publicity stunts in the funeral service, the whole deal."

More small talk. I take the bait this time. "He must have died young," I say.

"He did—thirty-one. Not as young as some—" Sasha cuts herself off, and I can feel the moment when she realizes what she's said, and to whom.

"I'm so sorry," she says. "I just love history."

"It's okay. I get it."

This place. It's all history now.

How will Joshua be remembered?

I reach into my pocket and touch the folded application. *He's alive,* I tell myself. *He has to be.*

Sasha drives me the rest of the way in silence. Yet as we pull to a stop, I suddenly wish she would talk about some long-dead star of the silver screen. Anything. For all my hope, I know it's just that: hope. And hopes are often dashed.

It's what they are made for: flying or falling.

My heart feels fragile, exposed. As if a knife tip hovers above it.

"You know what?" I say. "You can go. I need more time, and I'd rather be alone. Go ahead and tell Ty or Artie or whoever. I'm not hungry anyway. I'll see him back at the house tonight."

Sasha opens and closes her mouth at me like a confused animated fish with ridiculous va-va-voom lips.

"Here, I'll take care of it." I text Ty. Telling him I went sightseeing and that I look forward to meeting him later tonight. I show her the screen.

"I'll get myself home. Thanks."

I don't want an audience watching me look for something that may not exist. It's enough that *I* think I may be crazy. I don't need someone else making me feel that way.

She's already picked up her phone by the time I shut the door. Just doing her job, I remind myself.

A small breeze blows across my face, warm like a breath.

I push away from the car and wait for it to turn around and slowly drive away.

When I'm sure she's gone, I walk through the headstones. There's no one else in this part of the cemetery, but Birdies have left a trail of flowers and messages to the marker. It's not exactly hard to locate.

I read his name, the dates, surprised that there is no *beloved son and brother* or other such designation of family ties, just a quote from one of his songs.

One of his lyrics that was rewritten.

It's that more than anything else that makes me doubt my hope. That makes the tears rise. If Joshua were alive, if he faked his death, he wouldn't allow this. He wouldn't quote one of his songs at all.

That's Artie. Maybe Livie . . . but definitely not Joshua.

Tears blur my vision.

No.

I fight off the haze of grief. Deny it. Bury it in my heart.

There has to be something here.

I walk around the memorial. In my memory I place the white folding chairs and canopy, the officiant at the front, someone Artie found. And in the back there was a classical guitarist, Quinn's friend. None of the band could play— they were all in such shock.

I move to where my chair had rested, close to the front. Looking up across the cemetery I see the weeping willow in the distance. Whoever stood under its sheltering branches could likely see most of what was happening.

I walk around to the other side of the memorial and look back toward the cemetery wall. See where the paparazzi propped their giant zoom lenses. See the jacaranda tree where the cell phone picture was probably taken.

There's a crop of smaller mausoleums, to the right and back, between me and the exterior wall. It's hard at first to see the one from the other photo. The one with the shadow of legs projecting from behind it.

Then I see it, because I see the legs.

Two large stone cylinders stand to the side of one of the mausoleum. They must be for ornate floral arrangements, the type with giant stems and massive blossoms, like lilies.

I walk closer and study them. There was no one lingering here. No legs. Just the sun casting the cylinder shadows out from the edge of the mausoleum, making it look like someone was standing beside it, hiding in the shade.

Quashing the disappointment, I pivot and start the long walk to the weeping willow.

I duck under the willow branches and face Joshua's memorial. Although it's not exactly close, it would be possible to stand here and observe almost every element of the service.

I laugh, a short burst of sound, at the futility of being here.

Even if Joshua is dead, he's not here. He wouldn't be here even if we had found his body and buried it under his memorial.

It's why I've never made this pilgrimage before now.

A blade of grass is connected to the others all around it, multiple blades pressed close, connected at the root, touching above it.

Joshua's absence is like that. It spreads through me and touches every thought.

I walk out of the cemetery without looking back.

22

THE FURTHER I GO

use my phone to hail a car and ride to the studio in silence. I tell the driver to let me out in the parking lot of the fancy sushi restaurant next door. I get out and walk across the pavement, over a little divider of manicured landscaping, and up to the front of Aepolis Studios.

I know the layout well. Joshua recorded some tracks here when it all first started.

Back then, we went to producers instead of them coming to us.

In the front are several parking spaces marked RESERVED. There are no lights on behind the tinted glass front door.

I don't intend to knock.

I walk around to the side of the studio. A stone pathway leads to a heavy steel door with no features other than a small spy hole. Cigarette butts litter the ground. I pick one up.

All I have to do is wait.

It doesn't take long for the door to crack open. A young woman in a tight plaid jumper dress and thick-soled leather booties darts out. A cigarette is already dangling from her lip as she brings a lighter up.

I catch the door.

"Ha! Perfect timing," I say with a big smile. I flick the cigarette butt away. "Thanks!" I walk in as though I'm supposed to be there. Look like you belong, and people think you do.

I'm in the studio and down the delivery entrance hall in a matter of seconds.

I hear a drum set thumping, rattles and crashes. Then laughter. I follow the noise slowly, letting my eyes get accustomed to the dim light inside.

The studio feels more like a somewhat creepy theme park than a business. The hall leads to a lounge with brightly polished tin ceilings and dark magenta walls. Giant surreal artwork dominates the space. Contrasting colors spark on accent rails, furniture, rugs. There are driftwood tables, vintage Victorian and 1950s furnishings, overplush chairs, brass and silver and chrome, a riot of sensory delights— ornate, gilded, crowded. Velvet-flocked wallpaper to help soften the sound.

I keep walking. A woman's voice cuts through the silence. "It's been a long day, everyone. One final take and we're done. Give me your best and let's get out of here."

There's an open door just ahead and to my left.

It's a darkened room, an empty lounge with overstuffed zebra-hide furniture. Speakers line the wall. The only light comes from a massive window that looks onto the booth where the Ty and the band are recording.

In person Ty's makeover is no less jarring. His hair falls across his eyes in styled layers. It makes him look older. More artistic. Less dirt bike, more rock-and-roll.

I'm still not sure I like it.

His clothes match his hair—dark pants, gray T-shirt, heavy boots. Joshua 2.0.

Across the lounge there's a connecting door to a second room. Through beveled glass I see a massive mixing deck.

A beautiful older woman sits next to a man at the board. They are both intent over their slide toggles, making minute adjustments as Tyler steps forward to the mic.

I walk into the darkened lounge, feeling like a ghost of the past, watching through the studio window.

The drummer and bassist work together, a muted beat, the brushes on the snare and cymbal, countering the climbing, falling, repetitive slow bass, heavy like a tired heartbeat.

Ty closes his eyes, stepping up to the mic. He sings, just a normal voice, steady and clean.

Girl up in the air
Spinning without care,
The eyes of those below you
Know they cannot touch you.
Know they'd never touch you.
I let you fly away
I wanted you to stay

What the hell is going on? Lillian Leitzel. Again.

Ty wrote this? It doesn't fit him. But, again, only three people really knew about my obsession with her. Two of them are in that studio. Speed doesn't write lyrics; he couldn't care less about them. Never has. That just leaves Ty.

Or Joshua.

First, the college essay. Now a song about Lillian Leitzel.

Ty's eyes stay closed as he continues.

Once there was a kingdom
Not quite by the sea,
But you will always be
My Annabel Lee—
My Annabel Lee.

Something catches in my mind, like the flex and pull of worn metal. Subtle, but audible if you have ears to hear.

Annabel Lee? Ty hates poetry. I remember our sporadic phone conversations and overhearing his calls to Joshua after Livie put him in that fancy private school. He complained about everything. The uniform, the food, the classes, the teachers.

English was the subject he hated most, especially during the poetry units. He said it was b.s., a foreign language he could never translate.

The bass and drums stop, a split-second pause indicating the shift to the chorus. Ty pulls three simple chords from Joshua's guitar and sings higher, voice climbing and holding on the end notes of each line.

> *The further I go, the closer it becomes*
> *More I look, the quicker I succumb*
> *Stolen kisses—by the tree, a swing*
> *Your armored heart, the love you bring*
> *It will all be gone . . . someday*
> *It's gone, my love, it's leaving now,*
> *I would go, I would stay, I would—*
> *Go back somehow*

My heart catches and flexes, like the metal hinge loop of Leitzel's cuff, opening, fit to crack under the strain, the knowledge.

Joshua.

The swing is the towrope. The stolen kisses, referencing our first kiss and all that came after. The tree—is it as we left it? I have never gone back.

Joshua wished he could go back.

I don't need to hear another word, another note. All doubt has left my mind. I'm not crazy after all.

Holy hell.

Joshua Blackbird is alive.

23

FLYING OR FALLING

I step forward, into the light from the window.

Ty steps back from the mic and, turning to look at Quinn, sees me instead.

He freezes, abruptly stopping the chords climbing out of his brother's guitar.

Around him, the band members stop playing. They glance around in confusion.

How dare he hide this from me?

Behind the drum kit, Speed sees me, and his dark eyebrows lift in surprise even as he smiles.

"What's wrong? That was good." The woman sitting at the mixing deck speaks into her mic.

I hear her voice through the speakers. Just as I heard Ty's song.

Ty looks down, then he steps back, his fingers

tightening on the neck of his guitar. His head is tipped down, deliberately causing hair to fall in front of his eyes.

He's caught, and he knows it.

I glare at him. Words and feelings burn in my throat. I force my hands open and cross my arms over my chest, feeling a shaking starting in my shoulders. I tell myself it's not tears.

It's anger.

"Rox?" Ty's voice trails up. He glances up at me, leaning slightly away from the window where I stand, like I am a sparking bottle rocket, half held in his hand.

I could go off. I could take off his thumb.

"Okay, that's enough for today." The woman's voice. "We'll pick it back up tomorrow."

"Everyone give me a minute." Ty's voice lacks the authority that Joshua's had, but the musicians appear only too eager to escape the studio.

Even Speed, though he gives me another smile and a little wave before he follows the others out.

Ty turns and faces the booth. "You as well, please," he says to the sound engineers.

"That's okay. I'll stay," the man begins, oblivious to the pain and accusation radiating from me to Ty. "There's still a buzz under the—"

"We'll go." The woman grabs his arm and hauls him

up. She gives me a quick glance, then propels him out of the studio.

Ty props his brother's guitar on its stand and pushes through the connecting door into the booth and then into the lounge.

"Roxy, why didn't you tell me you were coming? I could have—"

I shove him, forcing him to take a step back. "Why didn't you tell me?" I can't keep the tremble from my voice. "That song . . . no way you wrote that."

Ty doesn't look into my eyes. He looks at my mouth, at my hands.

It tips in my head like ball bearings sliding across one of those old-fashioned tabletop-tipping games: turn the dials, slant the board, roll the ball around the numbered yawning holes in the deck.

Where will I land? What's the truth?

"Say something, Ty. Say. *Something.*"

He pulls his hand through his hair, dragging it back from his face.

I told myself I'd know. If I asked the question and looked at him, I would know.

Did I think I was psychic? That I could simply look at him and see the truth?

Ty just stands there, shaking his head. Unable to look at me.

Finally he says, "You're right. I didn't write the lyrics. I don't write any of them." He glances up at my eyes. Searching, not sure what he will find.

A question mark to match my own—and the parallel pain underneath it.

I think of the lyrics to the new song. My first kiss with Joshua—not Ty. No one else could have written that. No one.

"Joshua wrote it." My words are raw, eking out around the pain.

Ty winces. "I was going to tell you. Before it got released—"

"Tell me where he is."

Ty's eyes jump to mine, startled. "What? Where *who* is?"

Anger at being deceived claws at my throat. I shove his shoulder again.

"Then tell me who paid my tuition."

Ty's hands lift, palms open. His voice is sad, like he is trying to coax an injured animal. "Roxy, no. This isn't what you think. I don't know exactly what—"

"That's enough."

Artie.

Like clockwork. Like perfect-catch timing. Her parabola of presence timed with split-second perfection to snatch the falling moment before it can shatter.

"Roxanne." She smiles, but it doesn't reach her eyes. "I thought you were joining us later, at the restaurant."

She puts herself between Ty and me.

"I need to speak to Ty." My voice is tight. "Privately."

"Now is not a good time. Perhaps tonight. Now we have to go."

She takes Ty's arm and turns him. Ty's eyes are minnows, darting between me and Artie.

But he lets her push him away. He walks away from me without saying a word.

And for the first time, I think about what it must have been like to be Ty when Joshua became famous. To watch your constant companion, your guardian, your hero big brother, grow away, go away, and leave you behind.

What was his life like after his brother left?

A quiet abandonment. A sorrow no one else felt.

Then a tragedy happened, shattering and horrific. But unchangeable. After the grief, through it, because of it . . . It might be your turn to be somebody.

To be seen.

"The car will be waiting, Ty," Arties says. "I'll meet you in a few minutes."

Ty keeps walking away from me, down the hall to the doorway. Artie waits until he steps outside, and I catch a glimpse of a black SUV.

Artie turns back to where I stand. She sizes me up, caution in her eyes. Mistrust.

"Artie, I'm not crazy. What's happening—" Emotion

robs me of words, a choking that I can't express, not here, not to her, not when I can feel the grit-needle sting of tears gathering.

Grief and hope a rigging, forever holding me suspended.

Artie sighs and brings her watch up slightly.

Checking if she has enough time to say something consoling.

"Joshua had such gifts. Didn't he?" she says.

Had. Past tense.

"It all came so easily to him at first. But nothing about this is easy, no matter how it seems." She gives her manicure the once-over, and I watch the hardness return to her eyes. "I'm sorry I don't have any answers for you. Neither does Ty."

I think of Ty's face. The split second when I said the song was Joshua's. Guilt that then turned into surprise when I demanded he tell me where Joshua was.

Surprise turning into pity when he understood I thought Joshua was alive.

But Artie's face shows nothing. It's a shield, covering vulnerability.

"You know something," I say, not a question. An accusation.

Artie looks over my shoulder and crooks a finger.

I look behind me to see two huge security guys detach themselves from the wall and move toward us.

Artie's voice is professional. "I'm sure you can find your way out."

I laugh. "And here I thought for a second you were being human."

"Don't push me. Ty's security team is exceptional. They make Joshua's look like the babysitter's club."

She turns and walks away, heading down the hall toward where Ty disappeared.

I feel the presence of the security guards looming behind my back.

And that's when it hits me. I haven't seen Santiago. Everyone else is here, like a play with the same cast—except for the lead, of course. *Now playing the role of Joshua Blackbird, an understudy, Ty Blackbird.*

But all the other roles? Artie has made sure the rest of the group is precisely as she cast it for Joshua.

The show must go on.

Maybe that's why I haven't seen Santiago. Protecting Joshua felt like more than a role for him. Maybe he couldn't do it, after what happened.

It doesn't feel right. But who would blame him for not wanting to be part of this circus again?

When was the last time I saw him? My memory casts backward, seeking to fit Santiago's shape into the puzzle, a blur from days and days gone by. The haze of grief blurring the shapes even more.

But I remember. It was the memorial service, the drive to the cemetery, the circle of chairs. Everything beautiful and unreal, heightened into sideshow surrealism by shattering grief.

He was definitely there that day.

I close my eyes, trying to remember. For once summoning the pain, instead of burying it. Trying to remember anything beyond the white noise of shock.

I remember holding hands with Ty, with Livie.

Everyone crying. Everyone's eyes red-rimmed.

As we left, walking slow feet away, Santiago took my arm. He stepped forward, eyes downcast. He told me, "It's no one's fault. It's not your fault, Miss Roxanne."

I sobbed and hugged him. I reassured him it wasn't his fault, either.

He didn't cry, and he didn't look into my eyes again.

I thought it was his ex-marine stoicism. I thought he blamed himself even after telling me I shouldn't blame myself.

Everyone else came back. Everyone came back for Ty.

Why didn't he?

I sprint down the hall, crash through the door, and see Ty in the back of the SUV, Artie reaching out to close the door behind them.

Another guard comes at me, hands up.

"Artie!" I yell. "Artie!"

She leaves the door open, waves at me to come forward. "Make it quick, Roxanne. We're hungry."

"Why isn't Santiago here?"

It's almost worth her annoyance, the sudden startled shift of her face, wide eyes blinking.

"How should I know?" she snaps, recovering.

"You didn't try to hire him back?"

"Of course I did. He wasn't interested." She tries to pull the door closed, but my hand stops her.

Ty's eyebrows climb under the floppy fringe of his hair.

"You're saying you asked him, and he said no?" I still can't picture it. Can't picture Santiago turning it down, no matter what happened. I can't picture him saying no to Ty, even if he felt he'd failed his brother.

"That's correct. Now, if you don't mind?" Artie lifts my hand from the door frame.

I step back, and she slams the door. Through the dim glass I can see Ty talking to her urgently, frowning.

Artie isn't looking at him, her thumbs flying over her phone as she texts.

The security guard climbs into the front passenger seat, and the car pulls away.

Then they're gone.

My phone buzzes. A text from Artie.

Roxanne, breathe. For Ty's sake. Sending a car so we can talk in private.

I try to take a deep breath, but my body's not having it. What in the world is going on here?

Ten minutes later, a car arrives, windows tinted black. "Miss Stewart?" the driver asks.

I nod, and he opens the back door for me.

I half expect a ghost to be waiting for me inside, Joshua himself. But the car is empty.

The car follows the path that Artie and Ty's car took. A short drive, and we arrive at a posh restaurant, but the car passes the entrance slowly and turns into a café parking lot next door. We head to the back of the lot.

I stay in the car, watching my phone, waiting for instructions from Artie.

After ten minutes, my driver's phone dings. He reads the message, then unclips his seat belt, opens the door, and steps out. Just as quickly he opens the door to the seat opposite mine and Artie slides in.

"Leave us," she says to the driver before he closes the car door.

"Artie, what the hell is going on?"

"Ty doesn't know." Her eyes are sharp on me. "He doesn't know everything."

My heart is pounding. "Is Joshua alive?"

She looks away. "I don't know," she says. There is a crack in her voice.

"How can you not know?"

"Because I *don't*! I'm as surprised as you are to say it, Roxanne, but the truth is I don't know. A couple of days before the memorial service, a package was delivered to my office. No return address. No postage mark or any trace of who sent it or how it got there. It just showed up. No one paid any attention to it. There was too much going on. So the envelope was shoved aside with about a hundred others.

"The day of the memorial service, I went back to the office alone. After everything. I needed to throw myself into work. I went through the mail and spotted the envelope. Inside were handwritten lyric sheets. Joshua's handwriting. No note accompanying the lyrics. No anything. Just song lyrics."

I feel cold suddenly, the hairs on my arms standing up.

"They might have been sent before the night on the boat. Or they might have been sent after. No one has come forward. As far as I could tell, Joshua drowned that night and those lyrics are just part of what he left behind, knowing they would be·found."

I force myself to breathe. "You said Ty doesn't know everything?"

She shakes her head. "It's hard enough, doing what he's doing. Stepping into his brother's shadow, even if it's something Ty wants. So I told him that Joshua left behind another notebook. Made it sound like something

I'd known about. We're going to hold a press conference about it after the album comes out. But Ty wanted to wait until then, didn't need the added scrutiny. The added questions. And I told him not to breathe a word to anyone, even you, until he was ready."

Artie meets my eyes.

"But what Ty doesn't know is the timing or how the lyrics arrived. I didn't want that to hurt him. This way, it feels like a lost treasure found. A gift. Not something more painful."

I take all this in. It makes a kind of sense, yet it's almost too much to bear. If she's right, and this was something that Joshua did before the night he died, knowing what he was about to do . . .

Artie waits for me to process what she's just said. She takes a deep breath. "There's something more."

"What? Artie, what more could there possibly be?"

"That song you heard today. It wasn't part of that package, the one I found after the memorial service."

"What are you saying?"

"A few days after Ty's version of Orpheus landed online, another envelope arrived. Unmarked, just like the first. Inside was one more page."

My skin is going to explode.

"That's all I know, Roxanne. The end of the story. There has been no word from Joshua. No call, no text, no email. I haven't seen him since the boat." She looks me square in the eyes. "I would tell you if I had."

"And there's been no more mysterious envelopes?"

"No. Not since the second one arrived. I have no way of knowing if there will ever be a third. Or a fourth. As far as I know, Joshua Blackbird is dead."

"But you don't believe that—"

She laughs, a caustic sound. "I can't tell the difference between what I believe and what I want to believe anymore. When you asked about the college application, I have to admit it crossed my mind. That he applied for you. Paid the tuition."

"Don't you want to know what's going on? If he's alive?"

"Of course I do." Her voice has a sharpness I know all too well. "But it occurred to me that *he* may not want me to know. Think about it for a minute. If he's alive, then he arranged all this because he couldn't trust me with what he wanted. With what he needed. That he hated all of this *so much*—"

She leaves the rest unsaid, biting off the words that rush behind the guilt.

We sit in the car, listening to the soft whoosh of traffic behind us.

"So what now?" I say.

"That's up to you. No offense, Roxanne, but I really

don't care what you do. Go live your life. Go to college. Or don't—it's all the same to me."

Back on familiar ground, then.

"Except for one thing," Artie says, holding up a hand. "Ty. Let me tell him all this, when he's ready. When I'm ready. He's talented in his own way, and he's actually enjoying this life. I think he has the capacity to enjoy it all. Let him have it."

She waits for me to consider. I think about Ty and everything I never considered before. I think about being left by the two people you loved the most. Being left and having to find your own way.

Artie's not sunshining me about Ty liking performing. About him having the capacity to like this life, being famous. I could see it in Marchant when it started.

So I nod. Because it doesn't change anything for Ty. And it doesn't change anything about how I feel about him, or anything that happened between us.

Artie smiles and pats my hand like some aunt who doesn't really like teenagers. Then she opens the car door and leaves.

Not thirty seconds later, the driver returns.

"Where to?" he says to me.

I scroll through the day's events. One thing sticks out above the rest. One path left to follow.

"The airport," I tell my driver.

• • •

Ayudar is a tiny village of about three thousand people on the west coast of Mexico, a few hours' drive from Acapulco.

I whisper the word *ayudar,* pulling the sound through my tongue. It feels open, like a kiss. It means "help"—but I don't know if it means the place once needed help or that it now gives help to those in need.

The plane lands in Acapulco in the dark. I take a room at an airport hotel, and fall into an exhausted but short sleep, taunted by dreams of Joshua, images of him going into the water or smiling up at me from the boat deck, waiting.

In the morning I rent a car, a blue sedan. I've never done that before, but this whole trip seems to be about new possibilities. I buy a map in case my GPS goes out and then make my way to Ayudar.

What will I find when I get there?

I drive through the morning—pushing the questions away. I'll know soon enough.

Ayudar is as small as advertised. There's a tiny, two-street intersection in the center of a dust-blown downtown. A few thrift stores, restaurants, a grocery, some vacancy signs. A smattering of businesses. Beyond the immediate downtown are modest farms, a small school, and a hospital satellite clinic. An auto supply store and some gas stations and garages.

I drive through town, following GPS prompts until I have wound my way onto dirt roads on the extreme edge of town.

Suddenly I spot it, the white stucco of the house partially visible from the road.

I don't know what I was expecting. A small laugh huffs out because there's just a rusty mailbox, no name, just *#14* on it, and a dirt drive, heat cracked, threading down into a tangle of palm trees, mimosas, and bromeliads, all protected by a rough fence.

Across the driveway are two fat wires, stretched and hooked into a loop hanging off a post.

"Now what?" I whisper to myself. "You came all this way—what's a little trespassing?"

The car chimes as I open the door. I walk up to the stretched-wire fence, not certain if I'm moving slowly from fear or stiffness.

It takes a fair bit of strength to pull the wires over enough to unhook them. Carefully I drag them across the road, curling them on the dirt. I drive the car through and park on the other side and replace the wire gate, wondering if the fence is to keep strangers out or animals in.

"Don't get shot," I tell myself. "Drive like a friendly person."

Whatever that looks like.

The driveway winds down and around to the house. A battered Jeep is parked to the side. I park beside it and get out. Looking toward the front door, I see a curtain fall back into place behind a window.

I go to the door. Before I can knock, it opens.

Santiago looks out at me, the frown crease between his eyebrows battling against the reflexive smile on his mouth.

Before I can say anything, before I can greet him or glare at him and speak a word of accusation about Joshua's lyrics, he mutters something in Spanish and pulls me into a fierce hug.

I hug him back, surprised and not surprised to find how it makes me feel: safe and sound.

"Ah, Roxanne." Santiago's voice is a deep rumble against my ear. "It's good to see you."

"You too, Santi." But my voice drops into firmness, driven down by my hurt and anger. My eyes must match my voice, because Santiago steps back slightly. Then he nods.

"Better come inside." Santiago's eyes dart around, a habitual check from his days spent locating long-distance lenses. Then he sighs like he knows what's coming from me, but he opens the door wide anyway.

The house is tidy, wide wood and tile floors create

an echoing space. No jumble of knickknacks, no art or artifacts, just cool white walls and room all around you. A hallway leads to other rooms on the left, an arched doorway to the right connects to an empty dining room and probably a kitchen beyond that.

Weathered furniture presses back against the walls, almost hesitant to intrude.

Santiago gestures to a sofa, but I remain standing in the center of the room. His arm drops, and the frown returns, clouding his face.

"I know why you're here," he begins.

"How much more do you have?" I ask, my question an acid knot rising in my throat. "How many other lyric sheets? Did you take them and just decide to keep them?"

I step forward, making him improbably step back, this mountain of a man, retreating before my anger.

"Or is he alive?" Tears jump to my eyes. "Do you have any idea how crazy I feel even thinking that?"

His eyes are sad. He shakes his head at me. His mouth starts to move into the shapes that will say what I fear in my bones.

He will say the words that break me. A jumble of barbed wire tangles in my chest.

Santiago puts his hands up. "Oh, *mi niña*—"

"Tell me."

Santiago's eyes move around the room like the right words to say will form in giant letters on the bare expanse of walls around us.

"Tell me what's going on, Santiago. Tell me!"

I step forward again, another step away from the front door, away from the hallway behind me, pressing Santiago backward.

Something stirs the air. An infinitesimal change, the smallest of sparks. A feeling like being watched or of nearness, the feeling of dawning comprehension, when you hear the metal link snap.

The fine hairs on the back of my neck rise and stretch outward, uncanny seeking. Innate knowing.

I hear the voice as I turn.

"I'm so sorry, Rox."

Joshua stands behind me, close enough to touch. His hair is longer, grown out. His skin has lost its pallor, sun-warmed into health.

Changeable green eyes, fringed by those impossible lashes, stare at me, waiting.

My heart stops. And my breath. I feel my eyes go wide, drinking him in, afraid to blink. Afraid to move or startle the ghost of him away.

Too hungry for the sight of him to take the chance that he might disappear.

Shock courses through my body, a bolt that signals

and fires, signals and fires, reality and unreality, overlaying each other like an X-ray of bones beneath flesh. In my head, a swimming headache, confusion. My vision blurs, and I blink rapidly, tears slip out, and he's still there. Watching me. Waiting for me.

A sound like a laugh and like a cry wrings out of my chest.

Joshua is standing here.

Joshua is alive.

Alive! Alive! Alive! my brain chatters.

I step toward him. My knees wobble as adrenaline dumps in and recedes like a wave, pulling solid ground out from under me.

I stumble.

Joshua steps in quickly, closing the small distance between us. His movement is smooth, seamless as a perfect dream. He catches me, steadies me where I stand.

His scent envelops me. A smell of cheap white soap over a slight skin spice, some hint of tang that is wholly him.

A scent-triggered memory: me holding him tight. Pushing my nose into the skin behind his ear, breathing him in. Committing him to memory.

His callused hands hold my upper arms. Warmth radiates from his skin. Concrete. Real. Alive.

Joshua.

"You're alive." My voice is faint, suspended.

"Yes." Joshua's eyes change, regret, the flicker of the haunted expression he always wore after becoming *Joshua Blackbird*.

Then he smiles at me, sorrow and apology, and the reflected warmth that is mine. The smile from Marchant. From the first day we met. From the first day in class. A smile I learned and always knew was only for me.

I don't care about anything else. About the lyrics, the university, or how he is here, alive. About what Ty or Artie knows, or doesn't want to know.

None of it matters.

Joy surges through me, singing at every joint and synapse. Joy and heartfelt wonder. A love that burns and stings and heals, pulling me up by the wrist. Pulling me up into the air, into the sky. I am weightless, free from grief.

My arms lift, and I'm pulling him into me, pulling his head down, pressing our bodies together.

Joshua laughs, a familiar and foreign sound, something from a country where we lived long ago. He pulls on me as I pull on him. Our arms can't stop pressing, embracing. Our hands pass over each other in desperate, joyful recognition of solidity.

This is real.

Joshua kisses my cheeks, my eyelids, my forehead, my nose. Words burble out of my mouth in breathless gasps.

Words of love and astonishment and gratitude that he's here, alive, that we're here together.

Our lips meet, and the kiss catches us, holds us. An impossible rescue. Without stopping the kiss, I pull air from his lungs, pull his breath into me, and hold it there.

The link reknits itself. The apparatus holds.

We hold each other, clinging like strands are woven between us, a net to catch every breath. Every pain assuaged, every beauty marveled.

Joshua Blackbird is alive.

24

JOSHUA'S STORY

Santiago disappeared sometime during our reunion, reappearing only to hug me again and apologize. For keeping the secret, for not knowing what to say when I confronted him.

My emotions churn like the wake from a boat engine, the white foam of joy covering dark waters of hurt and anger.

But the accusing words stop behind my teeth every time I look at Joshua, his lithe frame beside mine, his face beautiful, a heart-catch smile. The dark clouds that covered him, the fear and exhaustion, are gone. All of it, vanished. He's Shu again.

Restored, replenished. Reinvented.

He is the same, and he's changed completely.

Joshua leads me through the white stucco house out

onto a sun-sheltered patio. Winding down and away from the back of the house is a dirt path that leads to a small private beach with the expanse of ocean beyond.

The patio is furnished sparely, just like the house. There's a low wood table and chairs with cushions in muted colors. An antique pierced-metal glider, spray painted with ocher, stands to the side, in the shade of a leaning fig tree.

"You—" The words stop again. I am so tired, but a need to know, to accuse, gathers like a sudden infection. "How could you?"

My need to know is fueled by anger and hope equally. Anger at being tricked, being cheated into feeling the pain of losing him. Anger buoyed and softened by the hope of forgiveness, of wanting to allow myself the gift of forgiveness, a feeling like my heart has let go and hangs there in empty air, waiting for the arc of the jump to resolve the moment. Will it fall or will it catch the swinging bar—

Or will it be caught by another's grip?

Sorrow colors Joshua's expressive face.

Had I forgotten how my eyes love to look at him?

My voice won't come, caught in the fear of falling.

Joshua's head tips to the side, a cringe of apology. He jams his hands into his pockets. "I'm sorry I hurt you." He clears his throat. "It's not enough to say it. I know that. But I *am* sorry."

I want to laugh. It's so profoundly surreal, I could almost expect the tree to start talking. Or for birds to fly to us bearing a wreath of flowers.

He's alive. He's alive, and he's standing here in front of me.

He let me think he was dead. He *wanted* me to think he was dead.

My heart falls.

"You're *sorry*." My voice is angry, angrier than I realized.

"I am, Rox. I'm so sorry. But I had to escape. It had to look real."

My cheeks are wet. Joshua's are, too.

"But I hoped you'd find me again. Let me explain. Please." Joshua looks at me like he's strapped to a spinning wooden wheel, and I'm holding the throwing knives.

"Please," he says, taking my hand, holding it gently. We walk to the glider and sit, a creaking sway of precarious pieces.

Joshua takes a deep breath. He looks out to the ocean as if its vastness will supply the words he needs.

"It felt like there was no other way," he says. "Dying started to feel like the only answer. And I don't know when that feeling began. Maybe it was after Dallas. Or before. It took me a long time to realize I didn't want to die. I just wanted that life to be over."

His voice falters; his chin tips down in shame or self-recrimination.

"At first it was like a promise I could offer to myself, That it didn't have to be this way. I could make it stop."

Joshua looks at me, but his eyes hold the expression of a hunted thing. Knowing the impossibility of escape.

The glider creaks, engineered to feel smooth but groaning under the weight of us.

"Rox, I didn't plan to kill myself. But after Dallas, after the first tour, and everything I grew to hate . . . well, thinking about dying comforted me. It felt like holding an ace, knowing how I could end it, end everything. I'd get a car. I'd drive out into the hills."

Hearing him talk about killing himself so casually rocks my head back on my shoulders.

Even if it's what I thought he had done before the university letter came.

Joshua's voice continues, telling the story of how he got here.

Thinking about dying consumed him, just as fame consumed him. It got to the point where it was always there. In Georgia, in LA, on the road; geography didn't change it. He couldn't escape, and more and more, he started to see how his pain was hurting the rest of us.

The rest of us were smothered lights, deserving freedom. Me and Ty and Speed, everyone who loved him. He saw how he was warping us, bending our light, pulling us into his darkness.

And the only way out that he could see, for all of us, was final.

"Then right before my birthday, I was talking to Artie. She was joking about being my guardian. Saying that I was too much to handle, and when I turned seventeen, I could get emancipated, just in time for tour. I asked her what that meant."

He shakes his head, a hint of a smile hovering at the corners of his mouth.

"She said I could spend my own money. Buy my mom a house. Buy myself a house. Buy a stranger a house. Do whatever I wanted as long as it was legal. 'Be in charge of your own fate' was how she put it."

I can picture Artie rattling off the possibilities.

"That's when I had the idea. I could arrange everything. Take care of everyone. Even me."

He could be someone else, and he didn't have to die to do it.

Joshua Blackbird, however, did. Because he knew he could never simply leave. Could never throw off the yoke of obligation, not as long as Artie, or the record label, or his mother, or anyone who wanted something more from him thought he was alive.

"That part took a while," he says. "Figuring out how to

try to make it look like an accident. I bought the houses, the land, everything, and I gave them away, and I tried to hide this place."

He gives me a crooked grin. "The house I bought for a stranger."

Himself, in the future.

Joshua stares out at the turquoise ocean.

"Did Ty know?"

"No." The answer is short. "But after Dallas, I'd talked to him, told him to watch out for you if something happened to me. I didn't know what else to do. Everything felt so wrong. Telling, not telling. I decided in the end not to tell anyone but Santi. He was the one person I never felt like I was hurting in some way."

His eyes glance at me, uncertain.

Joshua heaves a sigh. "It wasn't the best thinking, maybe. None of it. I can't say I thought about anything clearly for months, once it all started. Before I came here. But it was the best I could do."

So Santiago arranged for a small boat with a nearly silent, fully submersible motor. It was anchored in the island's lagoon two days before the yacht was scheduled to arrive.

On the night Joshua was to "die," Santiago went aboard the yacht with his own wetsuit, GPS locator and signal light, and a rope ladder. He went out his cabin window silently and swam to retrieve the small boat.

Joshua waited for Santiago's signal. A text message that he then deleted from his phone.

Joshua went down to the aft deck. Got a towel and left his shirt on the bench, trying to make it look like he planned to return.

Then he splashed into the water and swam out to meet Santiago, who waited in the dark just past the blinking lights of the dive buoy.

Santiago slipped out of the small boat, then returned to the yacht and climbed back up the rope ladder into his cabin. Joshua was safely on his way to a holiday rental cottage on the beach, already stocked with food and other supplies. It was only an hour down the coast from his brand-new mansion. He waited there for two weeks. Didn't turn on the news. Didn't leave.

He slept. He played video games on an antique console in the cottage. He read frayed paperback mysteries and listened to old music he found in a cabinet. Cassettes and records, bluegrass, blues and gospel, voices like a homecoming.

He slept, and he waited.

At night he opened the sliding glass doors and sat on the deck breathing the fresh, clean open air.

After the memorial, after we went back to Georgia, Santiago came in a car with dark-tinted windows and drove Joshua all the way down to Ayudar.

Sitting on the glider next to Joshua, staring out at the ocean, I can picture all of it perfectly.

The details are like a Möbius strip, where you can see the departure of reality, the twisting of what we all thought we experienced, how it became the inverse—life not death, a desperate grab at a chance, a loop to catch or a bar set swinging in a wide arc.

I don't have to ask why they undertook such a desperate plan. I don't ask why Santiago didn't come to me, or Speed, or Artie, because I was there. I remember a hundred lost arguments over time. The meet and greets stopped and then reinstated over Joshua's pleas. The tour dates that weren't cancelled, even after he was attacked in Dallas. The command to lip-synch over a prerecorded track at a New Year's event when he got strep throat. The endless string of nights when he couldn't turn off, couldn't sleep without drugs.

Fame like a strange servitude, the scales never square, the bill never settled, the demand never sated.

It's easy to picture what would have happened if Santiago had gone to Artie. The reason she's atoning for now, through protecting Ty and not finding Joshua. Because she would have intervened. She would have had Dr. Matt arrive with more pills. She would have tried to siphon off just enough pressure to keep Joshua going.

Because in her mind, it would just have been a moment

that needed managing, like all the other moments. Joshua was a person, yes, but more than that, he was a commodity.

And wasn't it every person's dream? To be a star?

There might have been pauses, but it would never fully stop. Not unless he made it happen himself.

I look at Joshua. The plea in his eyes, powerful. Seeking forgiveness. I look away from him to the ocean. He lets me sit in silence, absorbing his story.

I have only one more question.

"Why didn't you tell me?" I ask, and the words feel like razors.

"I was going to," he says. "I was going to ask you to come with me."

"And?"

Joshua looks out at the galloping waves below.

"I thought you'd be better without me. Have a better life. One that wasn't all about me. If I had told you, you would have felt obligated to disappear with me. How is that any fairer? How is that a life?"

He kicks at the bitten ground. The glider creaks and shudders.

"But after I got here . . . after a while, I wondered. If I'd done the right thing. If I hurt you more, or less by leaving. I didn't know what to do, didn't know what was right. So I sent a clue. Arranged for the university. Then I sent the song lyrics to Artie. And I left the rest up to fate, or to you. To your choice. But I never stopped hoping you'd find me."

Joshua scrubs his palms on his thighs, a gesture of nerves.

"I missed you like air," he says.

Suspending himself and me, here in this moment. Forgiving or falling.

25

THE HEART APPARATUS

We sit in the warm heat, motionless, like the world around us is a lung and we are a breath, waiting to be released into what will happen next.

Beside me, Joshua waits and watches me, his arms tightening to close around himself like wings of protection. But his eyes are hopeful and he offers a shy smile.

I think of Lillian Leitzel. How she always flirted with her audience. She would banter, pose, and smile. She wanted their love, and she got it.

And still there was never enough love for her.

Maybe that was the need that drove her, that made her great. The reason why she never could be content in her life. It was what her lovers and her husbands realized as their love was absorbed and she was never fulfilled.

Tragedies happen, but sometimes we court our tragedies. Make them wait with us, invite them in, like a vampire splinter, working its way under the skin. Riding in us like a parasite. Want and need never being met.

Lillian Leitzel, my Queen of the Air, courted her tragedy every night when she took to her rope. Twisting, climbing her Spanish web, making it to the top, where she would do her one-armed planges, swiveling and flipping over her shoulder.

She looked like a fairy queen at play, rising, over and over again. It looked like spinning. Like flight.

Every time she would flip, it dislocated her shoulder.

One night, the swivel snapped. The metal stressed and flexed to its breaking point. Leitzel fell. Her spotter had taken his eyes off her at that precise moment and wasn't able to reach her in time.

She twisted as she fell and struck the ground with her shoulders and head.

Although Alfredo Codona was performing at a separate engagement in Berlin, when he heard about Leitzel's fall he rushed to Copenhagen.

In spite of all their differences and the pain they'd caused each other, at the time of her fall their warring hearts had been trying to make peace. Each recognized the inescapable love they had.

I imagine Alfredo traveling across two countries,

horror in his heart. Just the report that she had fallen. As an acrobat, he would know, better than most, the dangers. What could happen. It must have played out in his mind.

He must have determined to mend the breach, to fly through the yawning air to her side.

But perhaps her magic would extend to her fall, a miraculous healing. After all, she had stayed conscious initially, and even waved away the stretcher, saying she could continue the act.

The theater management had known better, insisting she go to the hospital.

As Alfredo's train labored to Denmark, perhaps he told himself she would be all right. Perhaps he imagined comforting scenarios, imagined arriving to find her sitting up in the hospital bed, smiling, in a room awash with flowers. She might call to him, holding out her hand, her skin fair as peaches in milk, her infamous temper snapping out at the doctors who insisted she stay on bed rest.

"I'm fine, really," she would say, flashing that perfect smile, sparking life out of every pore. "See?"

That's not what he found. His Leitzel's face was bruised, discolored. Alfredo didn't kiss her for fear it would hurt.

She was in and out of consciousness, unable to speak, but seeming to recognize him.

Alfredo paced the floor, looking out the hospital window into the winter streets of Copenhagen. His heart was as foreign to him as this country, but with no neat rows of houses, no clean lines, his love instead a tangle of temperaments and childhood wounds, his love for her not a straight path, but a mass. Solid, snarled, clogged. It stoppered him.

He took her hand. So small and so strong. Their calluses matched, in palms and hearts. Tissues first broken and rubbed raw, then hardened. The numbing that protects from pain.

He waited by her bedside, filled with self-reproach. He should have been there. He should have caught her in his arms. He should have taught her how to fall.

Time passed. The doctors said the best thing for everyone was rest. There was no way to predict how long she would be asleep or if she would wake up, no way to know what would happen or when. It could be hours, days, weeks.

The Flying Codonas were under contract. Alfredo had to return. He boarded the train, wracked with fears and agonizing hope.

When he arrived in Berlin, he received the news.

Lillian Leitzel had died in the night, while he traveled away from her.

I think of his pain and her fears. She'd had a premonition, a nightmare of falling. But every night, her role was to defy death, to overcome terror and lift herself into the air.

Leitzel always risked. Always reached for what she

wanted, fought for it with every breath, no matter how it hurt. No matter how her shoulder hurt, or how her wrist was cut, again and again, skin torn by the cuff that held her aloft.

It was the price she paid for everything she needed. She accepted the pain that was part of it. Of everything.

Was that her greatest strength?

Joshua sits next to me on the bench, the glider swaying slightly in the shade of the fig tree. He's still waiting for a response. A reassurance.

He looks so healthy now. Here, away from the life that had wounded him, that dislocated him.

A mere hour ago, I thought Joshua was dead. That my hope he was alive was a delusion. And now I've heard him tell me that there were many times he *wanted* to be dead.

He had planned to kill himself. Not the night on the yacht, but before.

"Joshua," I say, and wait for him to look at me, "I need to know if you're going to be okay."

He frowns, looking away from me, out to the water. His arms tighten again, the reflexive move he's done since ninth grade whenever he's uncertain. Arms squeeze, lock across his stomach or chest.

"I don't know what you're asking," he says, one forearm angling up his chest as his hand works at the muscle between his shoulder and neck.

"Is this what you want? Where you want to be? You have to tell me, and it needs to be the truth. You owe me that much."

I see it suddenly, the wellspring of every problem we had, that he's ever had. Obligation like a contract of caring. Making himself fit. Finding his place in between everyone else's needs. You wouldn't think an international celebrity, someone who could crook a finger and get legions of people to fall over themselves to do his bidding, would have so much need. Or would have so much trouble taking what he needed.

But that's what it is. Joshua needs approval. Needs to be what is wanted. Needs to be cared for. Meeting obligation translates to his need to be kept safe. An if/then sum. If he can be what is needed, then he won't be left.

Even when I begged him to stop. My plea reduced by the sheer volume of obligation to everyone else.

Joshua pulls himself smaller, a frown pressing into his forehead as he looks at the packed-dirt ground.

"That's a hard question, Rox. There's a lot of things I'm still trying to understand. I barely know how I got here, much less what happens next. Being okay is . . . something you work for, I think."

"Do you want to stay here?" I ask.

He looks at me, his eyes seeking, like he's looking for me to cue him.

"I do, for now. I don't know about later." The words seem like a surprise to him. "I don't remember wanting. I just remember doing."

He slumps down in the glider, pressing his shoulders into the swing back, arms still clamped across himself. "I always loved the music," he says. "Performing it, writing it. It's what made everything else so confusing, because I love that part."

Another truth, and something that held him in place— loving music, hating what it cost him to be famous for it.

"I have a YouTube channel," Joshua confesses, suddenly shy. "It's just music. Instrumental, sometimes lyrics on the screen, but no voice. Stuff I write that no one would care about. And no me. It's not about me anymore."

It feels like landing safely on the ground and standing there with room all around. It's perfect. The fact that Joshua has this space for his music is beautiful and feels safe.

"That's wonderful, Shu," I say. "I would like to hear it sometime."

"Yeah, maybe," Joshua says, and the lack of confidence is new.

I smile at his uncertainty, at learning more about this new person I've known forever.

His arms uncross as he leans toward me, intent.

"Did I do the right thing?" Joshua asks. "Sending the

clues? Paying for your school, writing those lyrics? Or would it have been better if . . ."

He trails off, gaze reaching for me, hoping to catch, to save.

Lillian Leitzel accepted the pain that was a part of it. Accepted risk, accepted injury. Accepted all the mistakes and hurt between people who truly love each other.

I smile at him, and it's a clear spotlight of forgiveness, shining in the dark.

"I'll never be ready to say good-bye to you, Shu." I touch the back of his hand, longing transmitted through fingers and sun-warmed skin.

Joshua smiles at me, openhearted relief, and something more. Joy.

An answering warmth glows and grows brighter in my chest.

I remember how I felt when I thought Joshua was dead. I could rake him over the coals about how we mourned for him. How we all fell apart.

But I can't fully blame him. And I can't hold on to an injury when I can let it heal.

Our shared histories lie alongside each other like threads in a rope. Twining and pulling into a single thing. It may be frayed in some parts, stronger in others, but it's continuous. Fibers pulling into a strand that connects us. That holds us, lifts us aloft.

Except it's not a rope. It's stronger than that. Stronger even than a single snapping fitting, friction heated and cooled, stressed and breaking, leaving us plummeting, unable to recover.

Our shared histories and our love are a net. Separate, intertwining ropes woven into a safeguard. More than me, more than him, both of us with room to fail. Grace to fall.

It can be made stronger.

It can be mended.

Joshua reaches for my hand. Our fingers entwine, pressing together.

Forgiveness feels like flying.

AUTHOR'S NOTE

Lillian Leitzel (1892–1931) was the undisputed Queen of the Circus from 1915, during the Roaring Twenties, and beyond. Born Leopoldina Alitza Pelikan in what is now Poland, she, like the love of her life, Alfredo Codona, was part of a family of circus performers. However, she alone from her family had the grit, moxie, and charisma to make it all the way to becoming a featured solo performer in "The Greatest Show on Earth": the Ringling Bros. and Barnum & Bailey Circus. More than that, she became its central star. The first performer to demand and receive a private carriage on the circus train, she also demanded that she have absolutely no competition. No other acts went on in any other ring, and even more remarkable, all the butchers had to stop their calls selling concessions and souvenirs. She had the entire undivided attention of every eye, and she commanded it, a singular diamond shining in the dark. Leitzel had the innate ability to make the entire audience under the big top fall in love with her, from the sheer force of her presence and charm, before she ever took to the air. Like Roxy in the story, I fell in love with Leitzel's fire, her confidence, and her strength. If you search her name on YouTube, you will find several brief clips of her performances, including her famous planges. Similarly, you can also find footage of Alfredo and the Flying Codonas, some including Vera Bruce. His grace in the air is astonishing.

Stories about Leitzel are rich and varied, and oftentimes conflict factually. I attribute the differences to the innate romanticism of both her character and the circus. For the most detailed and comprehensive story of Lillian Leitzel, read Dean Jensen's excellent book *The Queen of the Air.* For further information on the history of the circus in America, read *The American Circus* by John Culhane, which is a treasure trove of performers, triumphs, tragedies, and all the vibrancy under the big top. Many other wonderful sources are available, both in print and online. Any liberties or errors with the histories of Leitzel and Codona in this book are my own and are perhaps caused by the combination of stardust and sawdust in my eyes.

I first heard about Lillian Leitzel and fell in love with the sprawling, glittering history of the American circus when I attended Ringling Bros. and Barnum & Bailey Clown College. LaVahn Hoh (professor emeritus at the University of Virginia) taught the circus history class at clown college, and it was one of the most fascinating classes I have ever had the great fortune to take. I am grateful for his introduction to the subject.

> *Friday I tasted life.*
> *It was a vast morsel.*
> *A circus passed the house.*

—EMILY DICKINSON

ACKNOWLEDGMENTS

To my editor, Michael Green, for story genesis and all the insights that came after, many thanks. To associate editor Brian Geffen and to the team at Philomel, thank you for your contributions and support.

I'm thankful to my agent, Jodi Reamer, for her guidance, wit, and encouragement.

My family's wellspring of love and patience is a treasure for which I am forever grateful.

For assistance with legal questions, I must thank my friend Tara Mann, Esq. Any legal errors or liberties in the story are entirely of my own making and in spite of her wise counsel.

Thanks also to Amy Heidish for LA landmark help, writerly commiserations, and friendship (again, any errors are all mine).

Thanks for the gifts of your friendship, inspiration, and help: Chantel Acevedo, Kara Bietz, Rachel Hawkins, and Vicky Alvear Schecter.

Lastly, a profound thanks to my readers.

Attending Ringling Bros. and Barnum & Bailey Clown College deeply enriched my life. I will forever be grateful to the circus and will carry "The Greatest Show on Earth" in my heart all my days.

Wellness can be a battle. If you're struggling, please do not do so alone. Resources may be found online at crisiscallcenter.org or suicidepreventionlifeline.org (1-800-273-8255—free call, open twenty-four hours a day, seven days a week). There are also many other national and state agencies available—check online or ask your local librarian for assistance.

TURN THE PAGE FOR A LOOK AT

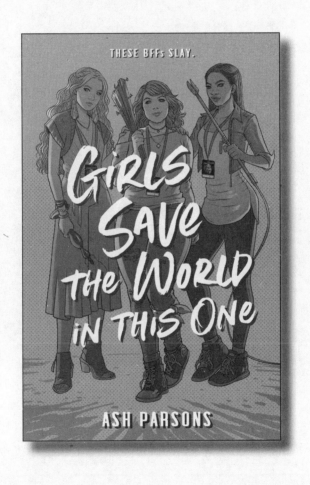

THESE BFFs SLAY.

Girls Save the World in This One

ASH PARSONS

1

We're never going to make it. This is it. My life is over.

In the days and months that follow this tragedy, when they speak my name, they'll say in hushed tones, "She died as she lived: full of complaint and bile, mere inches from her goal."

Mom twists to smile at me in the back seat.

"See, June? The doors aren't even open yet!" she says.

My best friend, Imani Choi, is riding shotgun, and it's good because this way my mom can't get the full force of my eye roll.

"I know they're not open yet, Mom. That's not the point."

Outside the convention center, there's already a snaking line along the sidewalk up the street and around the corner. A milling press of hundreds of early birds waiting to get in.

ZombieCon! is the biggest thing this town has ever seen. For the first time, it feels like the new convention center might reach its capacity, at least in the exhibit hall and ballroom. They're saying up to ten or even fifteen thousand people are projected to attend the con!

"Look at that line," I moan.

"I'm sure we'll be fine," Imani says.

I take a deep breath.

It's not Imani's fault we're not already in line for *Zombie-Con!* Even though we'd arranged to spend the night together, and said we'd get here before sunrise, and even though I'd texted Siggy last night to remind her again of the importance of getting here early. And even after I had set two alarms, and set my mom's alarm as well.

We're still running late.

It's Mom's fault. She laughed this aren't-you-cute indulgent laugh when I told her to get moving this morning, that the early bird catches the worm, the world isn't going to wait for you, rise and shine, all those nagging things she says to me every morning to go to obnoxious school. But now the one thing that I really want, the one thing I'd worked for, well, the one *fun* thing, and Mom had the nerve to say, "Hold your horses, I need coffee."

Then she moaned and complained, leaning against cabinets and counters, imitating me on school mornings. Paying me back for how hard I am to get going most mornings, and laughing like it was so original.

And as if that wasn't annoying enough, after coffee, and after Imani finished putting on her makeup (which she doesn't even need because her brown skin is flawless), on top of all that,

I had to listen to Mom ask Imani about the colleges she would apply for if the early decision one didn't work out. Which, I know, is the single issue that stresses Imani out so much, even if she's used to parents asking about it because *they all ask*.

Then Mom continued asking about other scholarships Imani might apply for (she's already got one sponsored by a local law office) and Mom kept going, *Do you know if Siggy is planning to take the SAT again? June is, you know that already, next Saturday, and maybe if there's time while you're standing in line, you could help quiz June on the test-prep app* . . . on and on and on.

I just kept quiet in the back seat. We were almost there; I'd worked for this day all summer, saving all my summer jobs money that didn't go toward gas. Between summer school and my jobs, my white skin barely even tanned, because I barely went outside during daylight, it felt like.

So I'm determined. Nothing but *nothing* is going to ruin today, not even the Math Booster app.

And not the fact that I'm retaking the SAT for the third time next weekend.

And not the fact that I'm not sure any college is going to admit me if I fail math again.

Someone has to let me in, right?

Right?

And not the fact that it doesn't really matter if I do take

the SAT again. My score isn't going to improve. We all *know* I have a learning disability. In math and math-y things. So why do I have to keep banging my head against this wall?

And not even the fact that there's a massive zit in the crease of my right nostril—and it looks horrible and hurts, too—on this day, this one day, when I'm going to take a million pictures and when I even have a coveted photo op with one of the stars of *Human Wasteland*.

The photo is the pièce de résistance of this, my first con experience.

The car line for the drop-off circle creeps forward, and Mom finally changes the subject from college and the SAT.

"Has your mom had a longer commute with all the protesters?" she asks Imani.

Imani's mom, Naomi, is a civilian contractor on the nearby army arsenal test range. There's been talk recently that USAMRIID (the US Army Medical Research Institute of Infectious Diseases) has established a field office at our arsenal, which would make sense if it's true, because Senoybia is also within an easy commute of the Centers for Disease Control in Atlanta.

But a lot of people don't like the idea of the army medical research field office on a test range, and so there's been an influx of protestors outside the arsenal gates.

"No, Mom says the drive time is about the same," Imani

answers. "But last week she dropped off two boxes of donuts on her way in: one for the protestors, and one for the military police at the gate."

"I just love that," Mom says. "So diplomatic and thoughtful."

Imani quirks a smile at Mom.

"Well, everyone also waves and gets out of the way for her now," Imani says.

Mom laughs and turns onto the road that runs along the front of the convention center drop-off circle. She whistles low. "Wow. That's a lot of people."

"I told you it was a big deal," I say, the words snapping between my teeth sharper than I mean, but would you *look* at that line?

"I know," Mom says. "I mean, I knew. But still. Wow."

Outside the car window, the rising sun tinges the silhouette of the convention center a pinkish gray, like a Hollywood backdrop only not in LA but here, in basic, boring, nice-place-to-raise-kids Senoybia, Georgia.

I'm not joking, they actually put that in the tourism brochures and on, like, the town website and stuff. Not that it's dull, just that it's a great "family town!" And stuff like "Slow down! Give Senoybia a try!"

It's a nice place, sure. But I can't blame anyone, Imani especially, for looking forward to graduation and college.

Our high school is like only 10 percent students of color. It's embarrassing how white it is.

So, I am excited for Imani next year, no matter where she goes, or how far away, because I know she's really looking forward to a larger city, and being around more people like her, black or Asian or biracial, and being in a town that isn't quite so Mayberry.

I mean, I'm looking forward to that, too! For my own self. It's just . . . I'm not entirely sure I'm graduating. Or getting into a college.

Anyway, it's a miracle that *ZombieCon!* is even here. I'm serious, it's like a gift from the fandom gods just to me. *ZombieCon!* travels around the country, but it usually only hits the really big cities. Your Los Angeleses, your Houstons, your Chicagos, your New Yorks. Not my Senoybia. But there had been a contest, with the tagline: "Is your city A WASTELAND?" that encouraged fans to petition the fanfest, and tell them why *ZombieCon!* should come to their town. I boosted the posts nominating Senoybia, and so did Imani, and Siggy. Blair did, too, back before I learned about what she did. When I still thought she was my friend.

Even thinking of her name summons a particular pain. Still new. Betrayal. This is what it feels like: shame, anger, and hurt, like sandpaper made of shattered glass, rubbing under your skin.

I shake my head to stop thinking about her.

Anyway, Senoybia won the contest, and our convention center was approved as the location. It's big enough, and new enough, and there's even a luxury hotel attached to the convention center by a skyway. I mean, they want you to call it a skyway, but really, it's a bridge-tube like the kind hamsters use. Ridiculous to even have it, of course, because on most days the traffic in downtown Senoybia is downright sleepy, sluggish, and otherwise nonexistent. A child could literally play on the street and be fine, most days.

Mom turns into the convention center drop-off circle and puts the van in park.

I have my safety belt off and the door open before Imani can finish saying, "Thanks for the ride and the spend-the-night, Mrs. Blue."

Imani and I get out onto the sidewalk. I adjust the neckline of my favorite olive green shirt. It's just the right amount of slouchy-and-stylish, with a wide scoop neckline that falls off one shoulder, so I always wear a wide-strapped black tank top underneath. Plus the olive color looks nice against my brownish-reddish hair. So that's a plus.

"You're welcome, sweet girl!" Mom puts the passenger window down and leans over to call to us. "Have fun! Stick together! See you at midnight!"

Imani gives a big nod and a little salute.

It's not Mom's fault she's hopelessly uncool. Or that she likes my friends and spends entirely too much time talking to them. I mean, I like talking to them, too, they're *my friends*.

Okay, but it was nice of her to offer to drop us off so we wouldn't have to spend an extra ten bucks on parking.

"Thanks, Mom!" I yell, and wave.

She blows me a kiss and eases back onto the street.

Imani smooths her crisp white tunic. She's so cool. She looks like a fashion blogger or something, her legs long and slender in black leggings, with sparkly black sneakers and a coral cropped jacket that matches her nails.

I look cute, too, and actually *feel* it. I'm short compared to Imani, and I'm not model-slender like her. I'm average, I think. Normal. Rounded. Some days I don't feel so good about my shape, but today I feel lush and curvy, wearing my favorite shirt, ripped skinny jeans, and red high-top Converse.

Imani gives me a smile, and I can tell she's thinking the same thing.

We look good.

Now it's really starting. I have a whole day to spend with my friends, with my fellow fans, with zombie and apocalyptic horror lovers from all over.

ZombieCon! The Ultimate in Undead Entertainment starts now!